A WREATH FROM BANGKOK

Gillian Sanders knew that her father needed help, but even David Chan could do nothing to help a man who was already dead. From Hong Kong, the murder trail leads to exotic Bangkok. Here, Chan hunts for an enemy who is his own match for speed and fighting acrobatics. Aided by Belinda Carrington and Tracey Ryan, he closes with a gang of ruthless art thieves who are looting temples and archaeological sites throughout South East Asia.

*Books by Charles Leader
in the Linford Mystery Library:*

A WREATH OF POPPIES
A WREATH FOR MISS WONG

ionally.

we left Connaught Rc
ou?"

we left the office block."

pulled her normally beautif

a grimace, and gave a w

her head that made her lor

ripple in a dance of flame

her shoulders.

young," I said. "Wearing

louse and a blue tartan mini

he has very nice legs, blue eye

ort-cut blonde hair. She look

teenage Julie Andrews. I'm sur

she had been male, handsome

y hairy-chested, and somewhere

Paul Newman class, then you

have been the first to spot her."

cey grinned, conceding that the

sional honours were even.

ell, at least she doesn't look

rous," she observed.

ll women are dangerous," I

med her firmly. "Especially those

may appear to be all sweetness

innocence."

2

CHARLES LEADER

♦

A WREATH FROM BANGKOK

Complete and Unabridged

LINFORD
Leicester

First published in Great Britain

First Linford Edition
published 1996

British Library CIP Data

Leader, Charles, *1938* –
A wreath from Bangkok.—Large print ed.—
Linford mystery library
1. English fiction—20th century
I. Title
823.9′14 [F]

ISBN 0–7089–7907–6

Published by
F. A. Thorpe (Publishing) Ltd.
Anstey, Leicestershire

Set by Words & Graphics Ltd.
Anstey, Leicestershire
Printed and bound in Great Britain by
T. J. Press (Padstow) Ltd., Padstow, Cornwall

This book is printed on acid-free paper

THE Dav
Agency i
floor of
overlooking a m
Hong Kong harb
be bettered from
The ride down to
smooth and brief, ₃
out of the elevator
moment of mild, m
We left the building
on to the busy pavem
Road, and after the fir
the first gentle prick
took another right turn
harbour, and then a left
artery of Des Voeux Ro
I was professionally cer
Tracey Ryan said c
being followed, David."
"When did you noti

conversa
"Whe
— and
"Whe
Trace
face int
shake o
red hai
around
"She
white b
skirt. S
and sh
like a
that if
possibl
in the
would
Tra
profes
"W
dang
"A
infor
who
and

"Why thank you, David. You really do know how to make a girl feel good." Tracey gave me her winning smile, but then paused. "Or was that just another of your ancient Chinese proverbs?"

"Number four-thousand-five-hundred-and-sixty-seven, to be precise. I've memorized the book."

"Spare me," Tracey begged. "Just tell me what you propose to do about this particular example of sweetness and innocence?"

"Obviously we have to find out who she is and what she wants."

Tracey flicked a glance casually at a glass shopfront that reflected the crowded pavement behind us.

"Well, at least she can't be too dangerous. Anybody who ever knew anything would never attempt to play tag in a blue tartan mini-skirt!"

We were passing a large Chinese department store with three successive entrances fronting the pavement on to Des Voeux Road. At six o'clock the office workers were heading for home, but the shops were still open and carrying on a lively trade. I paused as we drew level with the third entrance to the store.

"Stand and admire the lingerie," I said quietly.

Tracey obediently stopped and gazed thoughtfully into the shop window, while I allowed the human flow that eddied around us to jostle me into the doorway.

"Be careful," Tracey said, revising her opinion. "She might have a bazooka in her bra."

"I'll chance it," I countered. "I'm the original Chinese bulldog."

I heard Tracey chuckle as I pushed into the store. A shop-girl looked at me hopefully over a rack of garish neckties, but I shrugged and passed her by. I walked back behind the richly-stocked windows, past the central entrance only a few paces behind our amateur shadow in the blue tartan mini-skirt. She was standing in the centre of the pavement, a lonely little island in a stream of passing bodies, and biting her pretty lip with a high degree of uncertainty. Her eyes were fixed upon the spot fifty feet ahead where Tracey was apparently engrossed in studying the price tags on a range of exotic black lace scanties. I touched my hand lightly on her shoulder, and as though my fingers burned she jumped four vertical inches into the air. I brought her back down to the pavement and said politely.

"My name is David Chan. I believe that I must be the man you're looking for."

She spun round with so much agitation that she couldn't avoid bumping heavily against my chest. Her blue eyes were very wide and her shapely mouth dropped open in a distraught little O of alarm. In the moment of collision I felt nothing but the soft, swelling roundness of maturing breasts, so there definitely wasn't a bazooka in her bra. I decided that perhaps she wasn't dangerous after all, and resisted a strong temptation to apply my teeth gently to the uptilted end of her startled nose.

"I don't bite," I said, feeling that I needed the reminder as much as she needed the assurance.

She flushed a pretty crimson, and for the moment she was too embarrassed for words. She half-lifted her hands, but then allowed them to drop back limply at her sides. Then she looked back to where I should have been as though she still couldn't quite believe that I had in fact materialized behind her.

"I circled back through the store," I explained. "You were so long in making up your mind whether or not you wanted to approach me that I felt you needed help."

"I'm sorry," she began. "You must be — I mean I was — " She glanced over her shoulder to see Tracey strolling back to join us and words failed her again.

"This is Tracey Ryan," I introduced her. "Tracey is my partner — or at least, one of my partners."

"Hi," Tracey said, and smiled.

Our new acquaintance was still too flustered to respond, so I gave her time to gather her wits. Looking for somewhere to put her at her ease I spotted a *Dairy Bar* sign further back along the pavement. She looked a milk bar age, and with my hand still on her shoulder I steered her gently towards the sign.

"How do you like your milk shakes?" I asked. "Chocolate, strawberry or vanilla?"

For a moment she had been on the point of denying that she had any interest in us at all, but then she hesitantly admitted that her preference was a strawberry flavour. We entered the *Dairy Bar* and found a vacant table. I held out a chair for our young guest, and after another brief display of uncertainty she sat down. Tracey took the chair on her right, while I sat on her left. A waiter appeared promptly and I ordered three strawberry milk shakes.

"You still haven't told us your

name," I said as we waited. "That would at least be a start."

"It's Gillian," she said slowly, "Gillian Sanders."

"And you're English."

Her voice, and something in her manner had indicated as much, so it wasn't a difficult guess. She nodded.

"Are you living in Hong Kong?" Tracey enquired pleasantly. "Or are you just passing through?"

"I don't know — yet." Gillian Sanders looked as though she had almost regained her composure and then lost it again. She smiled faintly. "What I mean is that my father lives here in Hong Kong. I've been away to school in England. Now my schooling is finished so I've come back to join my father. I don't know whether I shall be staying permanently or not."

"So all your decisions are still to be made. That's an exciting crossroads in life." I smiled at her as our waiter reappeared with three strawberry milk shakes, and then there was a pause

8

as we bowed our heads and sipped up the first few inches of sweet pink froth through rainbow coloured straws. When I raised my eyes again Gillian was relaxed. I said gently.

"Why were you following us, Miss Sanders?"

Her blue eyes looked startled again, but only briefly. Then she removed her lips from the straw.

"I wanted to speak to you, Mister Chan," she answered simply.

"So why didn't you come up to the office?"

"I intended to, but it took me longer to find your office than I expected. I still don't know Hong Kong very well, even though I've spent most of my school holidays here. I know where to find all the cinemas, and which buses to take to get to the beaches, but I've never had to find my way about all these monstrous office blocks before. When I did manage to find the right block, and your name on the notice board, it was too late. You were already leaving the office. I saw you come out of the elevator."

"You could have approached me then."

She looked confused again. "It was too sudden. You see, I hadn't really made up my mind whether I was doing the right thing. If you hadn't appeared at just that moment, then I still don't know whether I would have screwed up enough courage to actually go up to your office and knock on the door. I held back — and then I just sort of kept you in sight while I tried to make up my mind to what I really wanted to do."

She looked at me hopefully, with no trace of deceit in her baby blue eyes, and I decided that I believed her.

"Let's forget that part of it," I suggested. "Events seem to have made up your mind for you, so now that we are sitting together and talking perhaps you should tell me why you feel that you might need the services of a Private Detective Agency?"

"Well — " She bit her lip. "It's difficult."

Tracey and I exchanged glances, and then Tracey put down her milk shake and adopted one of those conspiratorial girl-to-girl smiles.

"David is an easy man to talk to," she told Gillian, "But you haven't had time to know him yet. Now if it's something you can more easily confide in me — "

"No," Gillian said. "It's nothing like that." She looked at Tracey as though she was not even sure of what they were both talking about. "It's nothing to do with me at all. It's my father. I'm very worried about him."

"Then tell us about your father," I said gently. "Who and what is he?"

"His name is Mark Sanders," she answered. "And he's an antique dealer. He owns two shops, one here in Victoria, and the other on the opposite side of the harbour in Kowloon. He deals in rare objects of art, oriental furniture, Thai silks and gems, and all types of jade and ivory carvings and curios. His business has been successful, and I suppose he must be very rich. He sent me to one of the best private schools in England. We live in a villa high up on The Peak."

"You speak only of your father. What about your mother?"

"She died when I was eight years old. I suppose that's why Daddy sent me to school in England. He thought that I would get a better education and upbringing in a boarding school than he could give me here alone in Hong Kong."

I nodded, it sounded reasonable enough.

"Let's return to your father, Miss Sanders. Why are you worried about him? What reasons do you have for thinking that he might need a private detective?"

"I know that he's afraid," she said simply.

"Afraid of what?"

"I don't know. Something — or

somebody." She hesitated for the last time. She was not sure that she would be justified in explaining more, but to stop now would make her look too silly, and so she plunged on beyond the point of no return.

"In the past few days Daddy has been very tense and nervous. We have a rich home so he has always taken steps to protect it, but now he seems to be tightening up on all his normal security precautions. He's fitted new and stronger locks, and new burglar alarms. And also he's bought himself a gun. He keeps it under his pillow."

"Does he have a licence for the gun?"

"I don't know."

"Has he been to the police?"

"I don't know. I don't think so."

"Why didn't you go to the police?"

"I don't know." She was registering confusion again, but at least her face was only a mild pink. She had mastered the total embarrassment that had come with the shock of finding me so unexpectedly behind her. "I suppose it's because the police would be too — too official. I thought a private detective might be more helpful — more discreet."

I smiled at that.

"Miss Sanders, what exactly do you expect me to do?"

"I don't know." She looked suddenly hopeless. "I keep saying that all the time. You must think that I'm some kind of soppy parrot."

"No," I assured her. "But before I can offer you any kind of help or advice I must have some answers."

"And I don't know any," she said miserably. She gazed at her milk shake as though what remained had suddenly turned sour.

"Let's try again. You know that your father is worried. He's fitted new locks and alarms and he's bought himself a gun. Have you any ideas why he might be afraid? Can you make any inspired guesses?"

She tried to think, her smooth

14

brow creasing into unnatural wrinkles beneath the short blonde fringe. Finally she pulled a helpless face and shook her head.

"Have you asked your father any of these questions?" I persisted. "Have you tried to talk to him about any of this?"

"I did try," she said slowly, "But not directly. I didn't tell him that I knew about the gun, but I did ask about the locks and the new burglar alarms. He wouldn't give me any straight answers. He just said that he changed the locks and alarms every few years as a matter of routine, and that there was nothing for me to worry about. He didn't want to tell me what was wrong."

She stopped there, and hope filtered into the wide blue eyes as she gazed directly at me.

"Perhaps you could talk to him, Mister Chan. Perhaps he will talk to you."

"If he won't confide in his own daughter, then it's not likely that he'll want to confide in a stranger, not even a private detective."

"He won't talk to me because he doesn't want to worry me!" Gillian showed her first temperamental flicker of annoyance. "He still thinks that I'm his baby, who doesn't know anything and doesn't notice anything. I've been away so much that he isn't used to the idea of having a grown-up daughter around the house." She appealed to me again. "That's why I feel that he might talk to you, Mister Chan. I know that he's worried. I know that he needs help."

I looked to Tracey, but this was one of those rare occasions when she could offer me no advice. I had to turn away from the wry eyes of emerald green, and back to the baby blue gaze of our young guest.

"I'm not sure that I can help you, Miss Sanders. If your father came to me in person, then I would do everything legally possible to give him any help he needs. But you want to engage me in a very vague capacity on his behalf, which doesn't leave me with any notion of what I am expected to achieve." I gave her an apologetic smile and reached for my wallet. "All that I can suggest is that I give you my card, which you can then offer to your father. You don't have to tell him that we have already talked. Just say that my name has been recommended to you. You may have to confess that you've seen the gun, but I'm sure that you're brave enough to do that if it's necessary. Your father might be able to dismiss all your fears, or he might decide to come and see me. It's really up to him. I can hardly force my services on to a client who doesn't want them."

She stared down at the engraved card I placed on the table, but she didn't pick it up. Obviously it wasn't enough. She chewed gently on her lower lip, and then her eyes sought mine again.

"Please, Mister Chan, couldn't you just talk to him? I don't think he'd come to you if I only showed him the card, but if he actually met you — " She bit her lip with greater agitation. "I don't know who to turn to, Mister Chan. All my real friends are in England. I don't know many people in Hong Kong."

I remembered my bland assertion that even the sweetest and most innocent of young women could be dangerous, but even so I began to weaken. I sought for a compromise.

"I'll tell you what I'll do," I said at last. "It's getting late so I'll collect my car and drive you home. When we reach your father's villa you can invite me inside, for a coffee or a drink, it's the polite thing to do. You can introduce me to your father, but not as David Chan from the David Chan Detective Agency — I'll be just David whom you met socially in a milk bar. From there I'll have to assess your father's mood and responses for myself. If he proves friendly enough to prolong a conversation, then perhaps I can casually mention my line of business.

18

Then it's up to him. If he does need professional help or advice, then he'll have the opening to ask for it."

Gillian smiled her relief. "Thank you, Mister Chan. Now I'm sure that I've done the right thing."

"Don't thank me yet," I warned her. "All that I promise is to take you home."

She continued smiling and quickly sucked up the last of her strawberry milk shake.

"Let's go now," she said, "Before you change your mind."

★ ★ ★

I had left my car in the large car park in front of the Star Ferry Pier, only a few minutes walk from the milk bar. We climbed into the black Mercedes and by then it was dusk. The neon glory of Hong Kong radiated a soft violet glow into the night sky that faded only gradually into a distant, star-prickled blackness.

Above us, behind the glittering white blocks of Victoria, loomed the stark silhouette of The Peak, draped in golden necklaces of lights. I drove towards it, circling past the colossal Hilton Hotel, along Garden Road, and finally climbing up the ascending heights of Peak Road itself.

The higher we climbed the more panoramic the glittering view of Victoria, the Straits, and the opposite peninsular city of Kowloon became. The Straits were smooth as black silk between the massed lights of the ships at anchor, and the red reflections like stains of blood from the neon signs along the Kowloon waterfront. The two cities were a white maze of dazzling light and colour.

As we ascended above the city and the apartment blocks, the gardened villas on either side became richer, more luxurious and more extravagant, for up here only the very rich could afford to live. Gillian sat beside me to point out the way, and not until we were almost to the top did she direct me to turn off the main road. I finally stopped the Mercedes before a pair of ornamental wrought-iron gates set into a high wall, with beyond, pine trees, the scent of magnolias, and a glimpse of white walls and a green-tiled roof.

"This is it," Gillian said, a little apprehensively.

"I'll wait in the car," Tracey offered from behind us.

I nodded and got out. Gillian was ahead of me, opening the gates. I joined her and we strolled together up the neat driveway. I found time to admire the expensively landscaped garden, while Gillian nervously slipped her arm in mine. I had the feeling that I must be the first male she had ever taken home to meet her father. I smiled to reassure her.

There were lights in the villa, and a highly polished midnight blue three-litre Rover was parked at the top of the driveway. Mark Sanders was obviously at home.

Gillian led me past the car, up two broad white steps and into a semi-monumental portico where a spray of wild roses curled around one of the slender columns, a nice English touch in exotic Asia. She opened the door and we entered directly into a spacious living room with thick white pile carpets and blue drapes. It was a comfortable room, containing everything a man needed to relax, an extensive drinks cabinet, deep blue leather chairs, stereophonic sound equipment and a giant Japanese television. The prints, screens, and the exquisite carvings in teak, jade and ivory that had been arranged carefully around the room were a tasteful and priceless selection.

"Daddy must be in his study," Gillian said. "I'll go and fetch him."

I nodded and watched her cross the room. Then my attention wandered to a rich silk screen depicting two Thai dancers in colourful national costume. It was a superb work of artistic expression, and I was still absorbing the finer details when Gillian shrieked aloud.

I spun on my heel and reached her side in three seconds. She was standing in the doorway to a large, book-lined study, and over her trembling shoulder I saw the sprawled body stained with blood.

2

I MOVED Gillian away, gently but firmly. I didn't want to smear any possible fingerprints on the door knob, so I gripped the edge of the door lightly and pulled it towards us. It wasn't quite shut but it was enough to screen the dead man in the study. Gillian's face was white and the echoes of her scream were still vibrating in her throat. She looked at me with horrified eyes.

"Go back to the car," I said. "Run as quickly as you can and fetch Tracey."

She didn't know whether to obey or have hysterics. I gave her a push, again gently but firmly, and then she turned and ran.

After she had left the house I turned back to the half-closed door. I eased it open and stepped through into the book-lined room beyond. The desk light was burning, together with two red-shaded lamps on either side of the room. The man I presumed to be Mark Sanders lay to one side of the heavy desk. The carpet was crumpled as though he had fallen on to his back, and then tried to roll over and push himself up before collapsing on to his face. There was no real doubt in my mind, for he was too stiff and cold for there to be any hope of resurrection, but I knelt beside him to verify that he was far beyond any human aid.

He was a man of about fifty, with thick grey hair and a neat grey moustache. He looked as though he might have been a successful bank manager, a solicitor or a civil servant. In life he had probably been impressive, and up to an hour ago he had probably enjoyed good health. He wore a once-white evening jacket and a once-white shirt that were now stuck to his chest like rags of wet red silk. Judging by the blood, and what little I could see of his wounds without disturbing the position of the body, he had been very violently stabbed.

I stood up and glanced slowly around the room. There appeared to be nothing out of place. There were no signs of disorder, and no sign of the knife. While I pondered I heard the faint scuffle of feet in the gravel driveway outside, and then a sharp cry from Tracey. Then Gillian was desperately shouting my name.

I turned and sprinted back across the white carpet of the living room. The main door was still open and I went through the doorway, across the portico and down the two white steps in one long, leaping stride. Gillian was reeling against a flowering shrub as though she had stumbled and was only just regaining her balance. She pointed frantically to the corner of the villa, and the darkness that shrouded the garden beyond.

"There, Mister Chan. It was a man! Tracey chased him."

I continued running in the direction

of her pointing finger, and as I turned the corner I heard the quick patter of feet moving fast ahead. I followed the sounds, jumping blindly over more shrubs and flower beds, and ducking through the ornamental pines and sweet-smelling eucalyptus that sprang to meet me in the gloom. I realized as I passed the back end of the villa that I was running full tilt at an approaching wall, and then I saw the narrow gateway to my left. A shadow passed through the gateway, and then another, I plunged towards them, and as I passed through the gateway in turn I saw the two shadows close twenty yards ahead up the suddenly steep slope of the mountain.

The fleeing fugitive must have slipped and given Tracey the chance to grab at his arm. They stumbled sideways together and she hung on grimly for a few seconds before he made a violent effort to throw her off. I heard Tracey sob and gasp as the chopping sweep of his hand slammed into her stomach, and then she lost her grip and fell.

As Tracey rolled down the hillside I leapt lightly over her tumbling form. She had delayed our quarry for the few vital seconds it had taken for me to close the gap, and now he knew that it was too late to continue his flight. He had the advantage of higher ground, and so he waited for me with his body crouched and his hands spread apart. He was Asian, his face more angry than frightened, and his narrowed eyes glittered in the starlight. His threatening stance had all the challenge of a poised panther.

My own momentum meant that I had to rush him or lose the initiative. I did so, and he surprised me by pivoting on the ball of his left foot, his shoulders swayed back to maintain his balance, and as his right hip swung forward it drove his right leg in a flashing high kick straight for my breastbone. It wasn't the clumsy kick of a waterfront brawler, but the skilled and fluid movement of a man trained in the classic art of

Thai boxing. The solid impact caused me to stagger sideways, and then it was his turn to rush in on dancing feet, jabbing fists as fast and deadly as snakes' tongues at my face and body.

For a moment I wilted. He was young and agile, and although Thai boxing ranks as one of my own favourite sports he was at least my equal. I had to defend, blocking a series of hooks and cuts, and then swaying my head to avoid a straight right drive that would have exploded under my nose. As his fist streaked across my shoulder I changed the game, pivoted on my own right heel, and turned him over my left hip in a neat judo throw.

He landed well and did a controlled somersault in a small avalanche of rolling stones and torn grasses. Then he was up and facing me again, looking startled and annoyed, as though I had broken the rules. He uttered his first word, which I took to be an expression of disgust, in a language I didn't understand.

Whatever he lacked it wasn't courage, for he came straight back into the attack. For a few moments we fought fast and furiously on the darkened slope of the mountain. He was too nimble for me to get any kind of a locking grip on his person, and in any case he seemed to know as many tricks as I knew myself. We broke away and I tried to surprise him at his own game. I half turned my back and lashed out a swift heel kick at his solar plexus. The terrain defeated me, for a loose stone twisted under my braced right foot and I was off balance as I slipped down on to one knee. My opponent had also decided to abandon the rules and he kicked out neatly as I went down. The heel of his plimsoll-shod foot slammed me squarely between the eyes, and by the time I had picked myself up and blinked away the stars our violent encounter was over. I could see nothing, and only heard the last fading sounds of his passage as he disappeared into the night.

While I regained my breath and gingerly massaged my bruised temple, Tracey limped up to join me.

"Are you alright, David?"

"Only frustrated," I said. "Whoever your friend might be, he was a fast mover."

Tracey stared up the black, and now silent slope of the mountain. We were not far below The Peak and beyond the sharp outline of the summit the stars were brilliant.

"We saw him move away from the villa and into the garden," Tracey explained. "I shouted out to him, and when he ran I gave chase. It's a pity he got away."

"I think we both did our best," I consoled her. "He was lucky."

"He dropped something, though," Tracey said thoughtfully. "When I tackled him he had something in his hand, but he had to drop it in order to knock me away."

"What sort of something?"

Tracey gave me her practical smile.

"We'll know when we find it," she said, and then she led the way back down the slope to the spot where she had momentarily succeeded in coming to grips with our mystery fugitive.

I hesitated for a moment, still staring reluctantly up the mountainside. Then I accepted the fact that there was no possible hope of catching him, and went back to join the search. For a few minutes we moved about vaguely, turning over stones and pushing at small scrub bushes and grass tufts with our feet. Then Tracey made a quick movement forward and stooped down.

"This must be it, David. I knew there was something."

I joined her and she held the object up into the starlight. At first it looked like a large stone, but then I realized that I was looking at a six inch high figure of the Buddha, carved out of solid green jade: Some instinct made her handle it with reverence, and the same instinct told me that it was priceless.

We were silent for almost a minute, for the image commanded that kind of respect. I had seen and handled a thousand carved Buddhas in the handicraft shops of Hong Kong, but there had never been one that had affected me in this way. The serene smile and the cross-legged sitting position of meditation were all familiar, but what was different about this image was the feeling that radiated from it. I felt that this Buddha had been the object of prayer and worship for many centuries, and that it was now inseparable from the invisible surrounding atmosphere of veneration.

"Mister Chan."

I heard my name spoken with trepidation and turned to find Gillian behind us. She stood in the narrow gateway that led back into the villa garden, a small scared shadow with her arms wrapped around her breasts as though she was trying to huddle inside herself. Her voice broke the spell and we turned to rejoin her.

"Did — did he get away?"

I nodded apologetically.

"I'm sorry, Miss Sanders. He was just a little bit too fast for us."

She bit her lip. "Was he the man who killed — " She couldn't finish and became silent.

"I don't know yet." I paused, but she had to make the confirmation some time and so I asked her gently, "Was that your father in the study?"

She nodded, and then her face began to break. She was sobbing when Tracey moved forward to comfort her. I took the jade Buddha from Tracey's hand as she passed me, and Gillian failed to notice the exchange.

"Let's get back to the villa," I said quietly.

Gillian allowed herself to be led slowly and blindly through the darkened garden of pines and eucalyptus. When we reached the portico I stopped.

"Take her inside," I told Tracey. "And pour her a stiff brandy. I just want to make a quick search of the garden."

Tracey nodded and then led the unprotesting Gillian into the villa. I waited until they were gone and then turned and ran quickly down the driveway. I returned to the Mercedes, opened the door and slipped the jade Buddha behind the dashboard panel. I locked the panel and then made my way back to the villa. I didn't search the gardens because the police would eventually do that with their usual patience and thoroughness, and I didn't want my footprints adding to their confusion.

In the white-carpeted living room I found Gillian sitting silently on the blue leather settee. Tracey sat beside her with one comforting arm still around the younger girl's shoulders. Gillian's face was white and tear-stained, but at least she had stopped sobbing. She held a large brandy glass, but her eyes were blank and she made no attempt to bring the glass to her lips. I knelt beside her and touched her arm to gain her attention.

"Miss Sanders, I have to telephone the police," I said quietly. "Is there anyone you would like me to call first — any friend or relative that you would like to have with you when they arrive."

It took a moment for the question to register, and then she made a slow, negative movement of her head.

"Do you have a doctor here in Hong Kong? Do you know the name of your father's doctor?"

Again she shook her head. The tears made her eyes wet once more and Tracey held her closer. There were no words that could help and so I patted her arm gently and then turned away.

I went to the telephone and called my own doctor, who I knew would come out and treat her for shock. Then I called the agency office. Belinda Carrington had been working late, but there was no answer. I let the phone ring for a moment and then dialled the apartment that my two partners shared. This time I was lucky, for the phone was lifted and I heard Belinda's well-modulated, unmistakably English "hello."

"Belinda, this is David. I'm speaking from a villa at the top of Peak Road. You turn off along Garden Drive and you'll find the Mercedes parked in front of some ornamental iron gates. You can't miss it. Could you get up here as quickly as possible?"

"I'm not sure that I can," she said doubtfully. "I'm just about to step into the bath with a gin and tonic."

"It's an investigation," I explained. "One that developed rather rapidly tonight and has immediately turned into murder. The dead man was an art dealer, so your specialized knowledge might be useful."

"Murder!" Belinda spoke as though only that one word had registered. "David, don't do anything reckless until I get there."

"I'm the soul of discretion," I assured her.

"I wish you were. Is Tracey with you?"

"Tracey is here," I acknowledged, "Keeping a sweet, sisterly eye on all my little escapades."

Belinda sounded relieved. "Give me those directions again," she said. "And I'll be there as fast as I can drive."

I repeated her instructions and rang off. Only then did I call the police.

I returned to Tracey and Gillian and found them talking quietly. Gillian had swallowed some of her brandy, and Tracey had succeeded in getting her to talk about her school in England. I decided that it was best not to interfere and instead made a quiet tour of the rest of the villa.

I opened doors with the greatest care, and refrained from touching anything else. Everywhere there was evidence of rich living and luxury, but there was no disorder. There were a number of rare and obviously valuable *objects d'art* on proud display, enough to make any ordinary thief rich many times over, but they had not been touched. Everywhere was neat and tidy. There were three large bedrooms, one apparently a guest room, one obviously used by Sanders, and the other equally obviously used by Gillian. In Sander's room there were two very ancient and very beautiful Chinese prints framed on the wall. I moved each frame gently with a pencil taken from my top pocket, and behind the second print I found the wall safe. There was no sign that anyone had tried to force it, and in fact no sign that anyone had ever found it, or even bothered to look for it before me.

I continued my prowl, inspecting a lavish bathroom with a sunken roman bath, and finally coming to the one room in the villa that had not seen the conscientious hand of a houseproud servant. It was a combined store and workroom, filled with a host of antiques and carvings all in need of slight renovation. There was a workbench and a complex kit of tools, drills and a polishing wheel and a small lathe. It looked as though Sanders had not only traded in antiques, but also loved to handle them and even work on them himself.

I glanced around the workshop, and then my gaze rested on some fragments of broken pottery on the floor. I glanced around the room again, seeing objects in teak, sandalwood, silver, brass and porcelain, but no pottery. I couldn't see the object from which the pottery fragments had broken away. I picked up one of the jagged pieces, puzzled over it for a moment because it seemed out of place amongst the richer materials, and finally dropped it into my pocket.

I completed my inspection of the house without finding anything of interest, and finally returned to the main living room. Tracey and Gillian looked up expectantly.

"Nothing seems to be disturbed," I told them. "If the murderer was a thief then he must have lost his nerve before he could do any real thieving."

"*If* he was a thief?" Gillian spoke uncertainly and made it a question.

"At the moment we can't be sure. You did tell us that your father was afraid," I reminded her. I paused there and looked straight into her eyes. "Was there anything else that you didn't tell us?"

She stared back at me, and slowly shook her head.

I knelt beside her. "When you first talked to us you were holding back. You were afraid that you might not have been doing the right thing. Now there can no longer be any conflict of duty in your mind. The only way in which you can help your father is to help us find his murderer. Do you agree?"

She nodded dully.

I said gently, "Miss Sanders, what crime did your father commit?"

3

IT took almost a minute for my meaning to sink in, and then Gillian looked up slowly and stared into my eyes. Her jaw went rigid, and the real strength of her character showed on her tear-stained face. At last she said angrily,

"My father didn't commit any kind of crime, Mister Chan. He wasn't a criminal."

"Miss Sanders, I didn't mean to offend you, but we have to face some uncomfortable facts. You've told us that your father was afraid that something like this might happen. He was a worried man. He was taking unusual precautions to protect himself and his property. He had more than a premonition that he might die a violent death, and yet he made no attempt to enlist the aid of the police." I paused

42

there to make my point. "The fact that he didn't go to the police can only suggest that he had some reason for avoiding them."

"But he wasn't a criminal. He was a respected business-man. He made his money from antiques."

"Think carefully, Miss Sanders. Why didn't he go to the police?"

"I don't know," she said wretchedly. And then more positively, "But I do know that he wasn't a criminal!"

I decided to leave the matter there. The thought had been sown, and with luck she would think of an answer later without any further pressure. Also I had heard a cavalcade of cars arrive, and now the sound of brisk footsteps stamping up the gravel driveway.

I stood up and faced the door as they came in. The advance party consisted of two smart Chinese constables, a sergeant and an inspector, and two plain clothes Chinese detectives, all preceded by a stocky, fair-haired Welshman with grim blue eyes. He looked at me as though I were the killer pike in his favourite trout pool.

"Well, if it isn't Mister Chan. A murder was the report I received — what's it all about then?"

"I made that report, Superintendent," I said calmly. "The body is in the study."

The grim eyes studied me for another ten seconds. Then he crossed to the study door and pushed it open carefully with a forefinger. He stared inside for another twenty seconds and then returned to face me again. There was no point in waiting for the questions, so I simply gave him the answers.

"His name is Mark Sanders. He's an antique dealer. This is his daughter Gillian. Tracey and I brought Miss Sanders home about half an hour ago. She found her father's body. We did see a man running away from the villa immediately afterwards. Tracey and I gave chase, but we lost him higher up the slope of the mountain. We returned to the villa, and then I telephoned your people, and waited for your arrival." I stopped there, and decided that it was time to do the introductions. "Miss Sanders, this is Superintendent Ray Davies of the Hong Kong Police."

Davies looked down at Gillian and became human.

"I'm sorry, Miss Sanders. Truly I am." His lilting Welsh tongue had a convincing note of regret. However, he was a policeman and he continued. "It's not an easy thing to ask, Miss Sanders, but have you positively identified the body?"

Gillian nodded. "I was the first to see it. I know my own father."

Davies turned to the uniformed man beside him.

"Inspector Ling, get the men organized on a thorough search of the house and grounds. But until the photographer and the lab team arrive only you and I will enter the study."

Ling saluted briskly and relayed the necessary instructions to his sergeant.

The Chinese detectives scattered to explore the villa, while Davies and Ling entered the study. They closed the door softly, and left Gillian, Tracey and myself under the watchful eye of one remaining constable.

We waited in awkward silence, and finally I heard the sound of more vehicles arriving. Again I heard the light crunch of disturbed gravel, and then two new figures appeared. Doctor Cheng Yuo wore a sober grey suit and spectacles, and the black bag he carried proved a passport with the uncertain constable at the door. Immediately behind him walked a prim dream in sheer nylon stockings and an immaculate black and white check costume that had been tailored to match every curve of her beautiful body. Her cool, English poise was undisturbed, and not a single raven-black hair was out of place. However, behind the elegant golden butterfly spectacles there was a quizzical glint in the familiar hazel eyes.

"Miss Sanders, may I present Doctor Cheng Yuo," I said politely. "And this is the third partner in the David Chan Detective Agency — Miss Belinda Carrington."

The Doctor bowed gracefully, and the girls exchanged words of greeting.

"Belinda is an art detective," I explained. "Before joining the agency she worked for the International Council of Museums in Europe. Her knowledge in the fields of art and antiquities is practically encyclopaedic. She knows the shadier side of the art world, the fakes and forgeries, the smuggling and the illicit trading, better than anyone else. I'm not suggesting that your father was mixed up in any of the rackets, but his business was in rare Oriental antiquities, and so I felt that Belinda's specialized knowledge might be useful."

Gillian looked as though she was still ready to rise up in protest, so I stalled her by balancing up the compliments.

"Incidentally, Tracey is our narcotics

expert. She spent four years with the American F.B.I. With their individual talents and my local knowledge, I can confidently state that we compromise the most efficient private detective agency in Hong Kong."

The conversation got no further, for at that point the police pathologist and a forensic team arrived. The photographer who accompanied them managed to bang his tripod as he struggled through the doorway, and the noise brought Ray Davies out of the study. The Superintendent listed the jobs that he wanted done and the newcomers quickly went to work. The pathologist and the photographer vanished into the study where I heard the brisk Inspector Ling take charge. Davies decided that we were worth some more of his time.

"Hello, Belinda," he said shortly.

"Hello, Ray." They were acquainted and Belinda gave him a sweet smile, which he pretended had no effect.

"Chan — " His blue eyes were grim

again. "When you take a young lady out on a date, do you normally take your two partners along?"

"I called Belinda after we found the body," I said calmly. "The dead man was an antique dealer, and this whole villa is filled with what appear to me to be very valuable and genuine works of art. I wanted Belinda's opinion. I also called the Doctor because Miss Sanders has had a severe shock, and I think she'll probably need a sedative."

"You did a lot of telephoning." Davies disapproved. "But don't try to avoid the issue. You've already said that Miss Ryan was with you when you arrived at the villa."

"Then let me clear up the issue," I said helpfully. "Miss Sanders was not a date, as you choose to describe it. Tracey and I chanced to meet her socially this evening. All that happened was that we gave her a lift home. She invited us in to meet her father, and we found him dead."

"So you chanced to give her a lift,"

Davies said sceptically. "You're miles out of your way."

"The view from The Peak is one of the finest in the world," I informed him. "Hundreds of people come up here every night just to look out over the lights and the harbour. They've even built a cable railway for the tourists. Tonight Tracey and I just felt in the mood to join them. We gave Miss Sanders a ride home on the way."

"You can tell that story to my youngest constable. I wouldn't trust him to direct traffic in his own backyard, but I doubt if he'd believe you."

I looked hurt.

Davies sighed. "Chan, you're a private detective, and this is a murder case. All I want to know is how and why you're involved?"

"He isn't involved," Gillian said emphatically. "We only met tonight, and all he did was to drive me home."

Davies looked down at her, doubtfully. "Where did you meet him?"

"In a milk bar. He and Tracey were together. I recognized Mister Chan from a photograph in a newspaper. I spoke to him because I've never met a private detective before. He bought me a strawberry milk shake, and then offered me a lift home. That's all. There was nothing sinister." She began to look angry. "Why are you standing here asking all these silly questions. You should be trying to catch the man who ran away — the man who murdered my father!"

"Of course," Davies remembered, "The man who ran away." He looked at me sharply. "There really was a man?"

I nodded. "Tracey spotted him trying to escape through the garden. She caught him for a moment, but then he knocked her down. I made another try at holding him, but he gave me the slip on the mountainside."

"He gave you the slip!" Davies raised

a dubious eyebrow. "After all that hard, daily training at Sunny Cheong's gym you let one man give you the slip when you've actually got your hands on him? Chan, your reputation is going to suffer!"

"He was fast and he was good. I'd say he trained regularly on his own account. This time he was also lucky."

"Chinese?"

"No. His face was too round and too smooth, and just a shade too golden-brown. He spoke only once, and it definitely wasn't Cantonese or Mandarin, or any of the other Chinese dialects I know. He practised Thai boxing like a native, so I would suspect that Thailand is his home."

Davies looked thoughtful, but then we were interrupted by the sergeant who approached to make his report. The man carried a .38 revolver very carefully by the means of a pencil inserted up the barrel. When he had finished speaking Davies told him to seal the revolver in an envelope. Then the Welsh Superintendent turned to Gillian.

"Miss Sanders, did you know that your father kept a gun under his pillow?"

She nodded. "He bought it only a few days ago."

"Do you know why he thought it necessary to buy himself a firearm?"

She shook her head.

"The burglar alarm and some of the locks look as though they have only recently been installed — when did your father decide that they were necessary?"

"They were fitted two weeks ago. We've always taken these precautions, but my father said he always changed the locks every few years, and the new alarm was more up to date."

"But they didn't help him," Davies said quietly. "Somebody got in and stabbed him to death. My sergeant tells me that there are no signs that the house has been looted, have you had a look round to see if anything is missing?"

"Nothing has been taken from this room," Gillian said dully. "I haven't looked in any of the others."

Davies glanced slowly around the rare art works on display.

"There's nothing cheap here," Belinda informed him. "The ivory chess set is worth at least five hundred pounds, the silk scrolls are probably worth twice as much, while the Thai screen, the Ming vase and the blue peacock are probably priceless."

"A good haul for a thief," Davies said, "Yet the murderer left them all behind."

"Perhaps David and Tracey scared him off before he could get on with the job," Belinda suggested.

"Perhaps." Davies refused to commit himself. He turned his attention to Gillian again. "Miss Sanders, I shall have to ask you to tell me all about yourself, and about your father, and about his friends and about his business. Do you feel capable of answering all these questions now?"

Gillian raised a pale but steadfast face and nodded slowly. Davies pulled up one of the blue leather armchairs and sat down to face her. While they talked I could only wait patiently, while Belinda wandered idly about the room and examined each art object in turn. Gillian had little to say that I hadn't heard already, and Davies kept his questions to the minimum and allowed her to talk at her own pace.

"So you didn't really know your father very well," Davies said at last. "Most of your time has been spent at school in England."

Gillian nodded.

"And you can't give me the names of any really close friends or acquaintances?"

She shook her head.

"What about business contacts?"

"He has a Chinese manager to run each of his two shops, one in Queen's Road Central, and the other on Kowloon-side in Nathan Road. I know he also has good business contacts in Thailand, most of his best pieces come from there, and he promised to take me on his next trip to Bangkok."

Belinda had returned from her discreet wandering to overhear the last remark. "Most of the pieces in this room originate from Thailand," she offered. "Only the Ming vase comes from China."

"And the man who ran away was a Thai," Davies said. "This case seems to have a lot of connections with Thailand." He looked to Gillian again. "When did your father plan to take you on this trip to Bangkok?"

"In a few weeks time. We were — " It was all too much, and suddenly her brave front collapsed and she broke down into tears, turning her face to Tracey's shoulder.

"I think she's told you all that she knows," I told Davies quietly.

Doctor Cheng supported me. He had

been standing by for long enough and now he asserted his presence. "This young lady is still in a state of shock," he said firmly. "I will prescribe a sedative for her, and then she should be allowed to sleep."

Davies stood up, making no protest. "She can hardly stay here," he said doubtfully. "Where else can she go?"

"She can come home with us," Tracey said promptly. "Belinda and I can take care of her."

Davies had no objection and so it was quickly arranged. The three girls and the Doctor departed, but I did not escape so easily. Another half hour passed before Davies decided that he couldn't wring any more information out of me, and then grudgingly he told me that I too could leave. I paused in the doorway.

"Superintendent, have your men found the knife yet?"

"Not yet." He looked at me sharply.

"For what it's worth the man who ran away didn't have a knife," I said calmly. "He fought me fair with his hands."

Davies grunted thoughtfully, and I left before he could change his mind.

★ ★ ★

The girls had departed in Belinda's car, leaving me the Mercedes. I drove slowly down the mountain because I needed time to think, and when at last I arrived at the apartment my two partners shared thcy had already packed Gillian off to bed with a hot drink and two capsules prescribed by the doctor. Our guest was now asleep, so there was the opportunity to confer. Belinda and Tracey made themselves comfortable with large gins and tonic, and provided me with a scotch. We talked the case over, and finally I showed Belinda the jade Buddha.

"The young Thai I fought on the mountainside was very selective," I said quietly. "I'd say that Mark Sanders was dead at least thirty minutes before we found his body. That means that his killer had thirty minutes to search the house. He could have taken any one of a dozen works of art worth a small fortune, but he was only interested in this."

Belinda took the jade figure in both hands and examined it carefully. For a long time she was silent, and I noticed that she too handled the polished green Buddha with an instinctive reverence. Then at last she looked up and her eyes were softly shining.

"It's a wonderful piece, David. It must be at least a thousand years old, and it was carved with love. It's obviously of great devotional value. You can sense it merely by touching it. You can feel it — even if you know nothing of art and antiques, you must be able to feel it!"

"I can feel it," I assured her. "And so does Tracey."

Belinda gazed at the Buddha again.

"It could never have been bought on the open market, David. It belongs in a temple somewhere, and the people who venerated it would never willingly part with it. If this was taken from the villa, then I would say that to be in Sander's possession it must have been stolen from the original owners."

4

I CALLED on Belinda and Tracey at eight o'clock the next morning, and found that their guest was already up and eating a slow but adequate breakfast. After a night of deep sleep Gillian Sanders was dry-eyed and determined. Although still a little pale around the mouth she had made up her mind to what she intended to do next, and I guessed that she had already spoken of her intentions to my two partners. She put her proposition to me somewhat bluntly:

"Mister Chan, now that my father is dead I must be a very rich woman, I don't know how rich until I talk to his solicitor, but I am an only child and he had no other close relatives. I'm sure that everything he owned is now mine." She paused there to bite briefly at her lower lip, and then rushed on: "What I'm trying to say, Mister Chan, is that I now have enough money to employ your detective agency on my own behalf. I came to you too late to help my father, but I still want to do something for his memory. I want you to find his murderer!"

I looked to Belinda and Tracey who offered no immediate comment. Belinda simply handed me a cup of coffee and I sat down at the breakfast table while I considered my answer. Gillian stared at me earnestly over the toast rack.

"You could leave the murder investigation to the police," I suggested. "They are efficient, and they probably have as much chance as we would have of bringing the murderer to justice. Also their time spent on the case won't cost you a penny, where the agency service is expensive. Our retainer is one hundred dollars per day!"

"I don't care. Money is no object." There was a stubborn set to her face.

"I want to do something. I want you to do something!"

I regarded her gravely. "If we do accept you as a client, then we all have to be totally honest with each other — do you accept that?"

She nodded soberly.

I hesitated for a moment, and then went over to the elegant teak sideboard and removed the jade Buddha from the top drawer. I returned to the breakfast table and placed the Buddha carefully beside the silver coffee pot.

"Have you ever seen this before?" I asked her.

Gillian looked at it for a moment, and then shook her head.

"The man who ran away from the villa last night was forced to drop it when Tracey and I tried to stop him. We assume that he must have taken it from the house."

"It was never on display," Gillian said. "If it belonged to my father then he kept it hidden — or it only recently came into his possession. He

63

was always buying new pieces for the two shops, and often he brought them home."

"Belinda assures me that this figure has great religious value. It was almost certainly stolen from a temple, and that means that your father could not have acquired it legally on the open market."

Gillian looked confused, and then angry. "He could have bought it in good faith," she said at last. "Even if it was initially stolen, then thc thicvcs would only steal it in order to sell it. It could have changed hands a dozen times before it reached my father."

That was unlikely, but I decided not to press the issue.

From her reactions I didn't think that she had seen the Buddha before, and so I nodded blandly as though I accepted her argument, and then I returned the image to the sideboard. I sat down again and finished my coffee.

"Miss Sanders," I said finally, "The

agency will accept you as a client, and we will attempt, to the best of our ability, to find out who murdered your father."

Gillian smiled with an almost overwhelming relief, as though she had just won her first major battle in life.

I continued formally, "This morning you have to visit your solicitor, so I would suggest that Tracey should accompany you. Meanwhile Belinda and I will pay an unofficial visit to each of the two antique shops your father owned."

★ ★ ★

The shop in Queen's Road Central was easy to find. It was called *Exotic Art*, and was run by a young Chinese named Mister Sung who had two pretty Cantonese girls as his assistants. The manager was occupied with an elderly Japanese couple who were obviously tourists, and the two girls by a party of young American sailors, and so Belinda and I had freedom to browse. I followed Belinda's lead as we wandered about the shop. After five minutes one of the girls was able to attend to us, and spent some time helpfully describing the pieces on display. We finally left without making a purchase, and without making ourselves known.

"A lot of those pieces were modern production-line stuff," Belinda said when we were clear of the shop. "You could find identical pieces in a hundred other art shops. At the same time there were some very nice and genuine pieces for the more discerning. The bronze horse and the Chinese princess in pink coral were real collector's items. And the prices were fair."

"And there was a wide range of Thai silks," I pointed out. "Plus most of the precious stones on display probably came from Thailand, and it seemed to me that a large number of the carvings and the handicrafts were also Thai in origin."

Belinda nodded. "The Thailand connection does keep reappearing in this case. Sander's contacts there must have been very good." She paused "We might have learned more if we had asked some questions."

"We can always come back," I said. "If we had made ourselves obvious Mister Sung would now be telephoning his colleague on Kowloon-side. This way we can take a look at both shops before we alert any suspicions."

"If we can get there before the police," Belinda reminded me, and we both began to walk more briskly towards the Star Ferry Pier.

The ferry trip across the straits from Hong Kong island to the mainland city of Kowloon took five minutes lazy minutes. It was one of the most beautiful water-borne journeys in the world, sandwiched between a blazing blue sky and a dazzling blue sea, and because there was no way to hurry it I relaxed and enjoyed it. A junk sail hung like a painting in silhouette on the heat haze of the horizon, and a giant white cruise liner was pulling out slowly from the modern Ocean Terminal on Kowloon-side, only a stone's throw from the pier where the ferry docked. The short journey was over all too soon, and as we stepped on to land we began to hurry again.

The Kowloon branch of *Exotic Art* was half way along the main thoroughfare of Nathan Road, one of the most glittering and extravagant shopping streets in the whole of Asia. By night it was a blinding chasm of multi-coloured neon light, filled with a never-ending bustle of traffic and pavement crowds, and by day it was only slightly less brilliant. We entered the shop and again began to browse.

The manager here was a middle-aged Chinese with an unpleasantly fat face. He also had the hand-washing approach that had caused some Chinese shopkeepers to be regarded cynically as the Jews of the East. He allowed us a few minutes, and then came towards us with a smile.

"My name is Mister Wang. Can I help you please?"

I returned the smile. "We're just looking." I said.

Wang glanced sideways at the porcelain jar that had briefly captured Belinda's attention. The jar was globular in shape, glazed creamy-white with a delicate brushwork decoration of golden leaves and pine branches.

"This is very nice piece," Wang said reverently. "It is early Ming dynasty, a unique piece almost six hundred years old. At thirteen hundred Hong Kong dollars it is very reasonable."

"It's late Ming," Belinda corrected him gently. "Less than four hundred years old and certainly not unique. It's genuine, but I have seen other examples. At thirteen hundred dollars it's highly over-priced."

Wang was not offended, in fact he looked pleased. He accepted the jar which Belinda returned to him and put it aside.

"The lady's knowledge exceeds my own. I am grateful for this information." He paused. "Perhaps the lady is looking for some particular form of art?"

"I do represent a private collector," Belinda said, inventing on the spur of the moment. "He is not really very cultured, but he is very rich. He only demands that every work of art he buys must be rare and genuine."

Wang looked thoughtful, and made a point of studying both our faces. "Perhaps I can help," he said at last. "We do have a small reputation with collectors and museums for whom we can occasionally locate unique pieces. May I show you some examples?"

Belinda nodded and he led us to the back of the shop. There he produced a small range of art works for her inspection. There was an exquisite red-lacquered jewel box, a bronze leopard with gold and silver inlay, a rich silk wall hanging, and the slender ivory figure of a monk. Belinda lingered over them all, complimenting and discussing the merits of each one. Wang offered nothing else, and finally she begged time to think the matter over. Wang concealed his disappointment behind a polite mask as we left the shop.

"What's your verdict?" I asked, as we strolled back at a more leisurely pace along Nathan Road.

"I didn't like him," Belinda said promptly. "Mister Wang was far too smooth and oily for my taste. However, the pieces he showed me were all good quality, and an interesting point is that except for the jewel box they all came from Thailand. Also I had the feeling that he was holding something back."

"Can you explain that more precisely?"

Belinda frowned. "I don't know, David. When I told him that story about representing a private collector he showed a moment of positive interest. Then somewhere along the line it seemed as though I failed to continue with the right responses, and he either became wary or lost interest. I think he could have showed or offered us more."

"The pieces he did offer us — could they have been stolen?"

"It's hard to say, but I don't think they were important." She stopped suddenly and faced me. "David, you must know that there's a huge international racket in stolen antiquities. In America and Europe there are innumerable collectors and private museums creating a huge demand for such items that cannot be filled legitimately. The result is large organized gangs working in remote parts of the world, looting temples and archaeological sites, and in some cases systematically cutting them to pieces. It's a sad paradox that the poorest and most underdeveloped countries of today usually have the richest relics of a cultural past buried in their hills and jungles, and in most cases the natives are eager to sell them for cash. It's become a giant criminal carve-up of the past. I was working on this problem with the International Council of Museums before their finances ran out and my job vanished with it."

I understood. "Mister Wang hinted that he was in a position to supply a private collector or a museum with unusual pieces," I concluded for her. "And so you think that we may have touched on the fringe of one of the rackets?"

"It's possible," Belinda said. "I know that it happens on a very large scale."

"It could explain why Mark Sanders was so very successful in his field," I mused gently. "And it could also provide a motive for his murder."

"It is possible," Belinda said again, and then she offered a note of warning. "David, before we go charging off on the exotic trail of temple thieves, perhaps we should look more carefully at the family involvements in this business."

I looked at her curiously. "What exactly do you mean?"

"I mean that it is rather a coincidence that Gillian Sanders should invite you to the villa at just the right moment to find her father's corpse." Belinda gazed at me with the severe look she often used when she mistrusted my judgement. "Don't be fooled by those wide blue eyes, David. Gillian may have only just left school, but she's growing up very fast into a strong-willed young woman. She could know a lot more than she is telling."

Reluctantly I reflected on the idea.

★ ★ ★

We returned to Hong Kong, ate lunch in a restaurant, and then went up to the agency office overlooking the harbour. There was some mail to be answered and Belinda seated herself briefly behind her typewriter. At two o'clock Tracey and Gillian appeared.

"Any complications?" I asked.

"Not really." Gillian looked subdued and it was Tracey who answered.

"We had no trouble in locating Mark Sander's solicitor. He's another Englishman named Robinson with an office here in Hong Kong. He'd already had a visit from the police so we were no surprise. He told us that Sanders had made no will, so everything automatically comes to his next of kin, which is Gillian. However, everything isn't quite as much as we supposed. It seems that Sanders wasn't the sole owner of the two branches of *Exotic Art*. He had a co-owner, a Mister Srivaji who owns *Siam Antiques* in Bangkok."

"I've heard my father speak of this man Srivaji," Gillian said doubtfully. "I thought that he was just a business contact. I never realized that they were partners."

"It does explain why the two branches of *Exotic Art* are so well stocked with Thai handicrafts," Belinda mused.

I looked at Tracey. "Anything else?"

Tracey shrugged and sat one hip casually on the edge of her desk. It was a habit of hers which always distracted me with those perfect legs.

"Robinson promised to make the funeral arrangements and to take care of all the legal details," she informed us. "He seems to think that Sanders must have been murdered by a stray thief. I feel that that is a genuine belief on his part, and so obviously he has no reason for suspecting anything else. What have you and Belinda discovered?"

"Nothing," I admitted wryly. "Although it would not surprise either of us to learn that the Kowloon manager is a crook."

Tracey was thoughtful. "Now that we know that Gillian is definitely a part owner of *Exotic Art* she could insist that both managers show us their books."

"She could," I agreed. "But the police will probably be checking those books by now, and there is no point in the agency making an exact parallel of the police enquiry. I'm sure that we shall be seeing Superintendent Davies again, possibly we can co-operate. In the meantime we must think of something else."

★ ★ ★

Four days passed, and during that time Ray Davies called twice, to ask questions, and to collect written statements from Tracey and myself. Initially he was not as friendly as I had hoped, and it seemed that neither the agency nor the police had any real lead. I suspected at that stage that it was only the agency involvement that prevented Davies from listing the case as another routine murder by a burglar unknown.

Belinda, Tracey and I eventually attended Sander's funeral to give Gillian some moral support. Davies appeared unobtrusively at the graveside, looking for any unfamiliar face showing any unusual signs of interest. The funeral party was small, a few neighbours, Mister Sung and Mister Wang and their shopgirls, and a few business friends of the departed. At the end of the service Davies was the first to walk away.

We took Gillian back to the agency office. She had cried at the cemetery, but she was strong enough to recover quickly. I reflected that perhaps it was merciful that separation had prevented her from knowing her father too well.

"Is that the end of it?" she asked me bitterly.

"It could be a moment to reconsider," I suggested. "Our investigation has so far proved completely negative, and I'm beginning to doubt that the answers are to be found in Hong Kong."

"Then why stay in Hong Kong?" she demanded. "The man you chased away from the villa was a Thai. The police haven't been able to find him, which means that he's probably back in Thailand by now. And this Mister Srivaji who owns half of my father's business in Bangkok. Perhaps it was Srivaji who sent that man to murder my father!"

"We must not jump to conclusions," I cautioned her. "And you must bear in mind that it will be expensive for me to fly to Bangkok just to talk to Srivaji."

"Bangkok isn't very far, and I don't care about expenses. I've got the money and I owe it to my father to do everything I can. I want us all to go to Bangkok. The answer must be there!"

She was adamant, and because I agreed with her I finally allowed myself to be persuaded.

5

THERE were a few loose ends to clear up at the office, and so I was behind my desk the next morning when the doorbell rang. I answered it and found Ray Davies on my doorstep.

"Good morning, Chan." He was as friendly as a Police Superintendent on duty could ever be, which meant that he was no longer hostile. "May I come in?"

"Please do." I offered him a chair and returned to my own.

He glanced casually at the two empty desks.

"Where are the girls?"

"Belinda and Tracey are packing their suitcases," I explained. "It's normally a lengthy process."

He nodded. "I have been informed that you have all booked airline tickets with Cathay-Pacific — to Bangkok I believe."

It was my turn to nod. "Miss Landers and I are flying to Bangkok this afternoon. Belinda and Tracey are following on a later flight."

"Actually it was Belinda I wanted to talk to."

"I can give you her telephone number."

"I already have it." He smiled slowly. "But it's not that important. You were with her when you visited the two branches of *Exotic Art* — what joint conclusions did you reach?"

"On the surface it's an honestly run business. Belinda felt that there was the usual balance of rare pieces to the bulk of factory produced handicrafts. The Kowloon manager tends to inflate his prices, but that's a common fault." I paused. "Did the police inspection of their books reveal anything?"

"There were no discrepancies. The books are all in order." He paused, and gently massaged the lobe of his left ear between his finger and thumb. It was an unconscious action which meant that he was thoughtful. "What interests me is the unusual number of very rare art works at the villa. I suspect that some of them might have been impossible to obtain on the legal market. Did Belinda have any ideas?"

We were being unusually cooperative, so I told him about Mister Wang's hinted ability to supply rare items to private buyers, together with Belinda's subsequent musings on the international art rackets.

"The kind of gang we're thinking of couldn't operate inside Communist China," Davies said. "And there's a marked lack of archaeological sites and remote temples in the New Territories. Is that why you're going to Thailand?"

"It's one reason," I admitted. "The others are that Sanders had a silent partner in Bangkok, and the man who ran away from the villa was a Thai." I was being deliberately helpful in the hope of some return favour, and finally asked. "Did the police learn anything from the villa?"

"Very little. There was no sign of the knife that killed Sanders, and there were no fingerprints. I might be inclined to believe that Sanders disturbed a sneak thief, and that you then frightened our thief-turned-murderer away — except for two puzzling little points."

"Go on," I prompted gently.

The blue eyes smiled at me, and the musical Welsh voice became more pronounced as he relaxed. "Chan, you're going to Thailand, and I think you might be on the right track. Bangkok is a long way off my beat, so we won't be getting in each other's hair. And because I want this case cleared up I'll tell you a couple of points that you may have missed. The time of death established by our pathologist indicates that Sanders was dead at least forty minutes before you arrived at the villa. The events of those forty minutes are a complete mystery, and the murderer and the man you disturbed may not necessarily have been the same man. The second point is that despite all his precautions, the gun and the locks and the alarm, Sanders still fell an easy victim to his killer. That suggests to me that even though he had some cause to be frightened he had relaxed and dropped his guard. The killer could have been someone he knew and trusted."

"Thank you, Superintendent," I said quietly. "I'll bear all that in mind."

He hadn't told me anything that had not occurred to me before, but it was nice to know that we were on sociable terms for a change.

★ ★ ★

Later that afternoon Belinda and Tracey drove Gillian and I out to Kai Tak Airport, where we boarded the giant Convair Coronado jet of Cathay-Pacific Airlines. My two partners waved us a temporary farewell as the jet thundered down the single runway

84

that thrust straight out to sea. On either side cargo ships flashed by in a disconcerting blur of motion, and when the runway ended it seemed that we must plunge into the blue water to join them. Then the Coronado leaned backwards and climbed up into the equally blue sky. We circled above the Kowloon Peninsular, the harbour and the islands of Hong Kong, and at twenty thousand feet the aircraft found a level course and cruised south east at six hundred miles per hour.

The flight lasted for two hours and fifteen minutes, during which an attractive air hostess served coffee and a light meal. During the rest of the flight I browsed through magazines, while Gillian gazed out at the impressive skyscape of tumbled white cloud formations beyond the great silver curve of the wing.

We landed on schedule at Bangkok's Don Muang Airport, sweeping in over the winding course of the great Menam Chao Phya River, and the fertile green fields and palm groves that were once the delta of the Gulf Of Siam. By now the cloud banks had disappeared over the China Sea, and the Coronado dropped gracefully out of an inverted bowl of eye-searing blue. When we stepped out of the fuselage door and descended the gangway I found the temperature much more sweltering than the comfortable sunshine we had left behind in Hong Kong.

The customs formalities were friendly and brief, and I felt the cheerful warmth of the Thai nature that even affected their officials. A smiling girl showed us to the airport bus, and soon we were moving again on the last twenty miles of the journey into the city. The road was a fast, straight dual carriageway, with on either side flat and peaceful green fields. It seemed that here the only possible hazard to life and limb must be the reckless orange buses of the public transport system which flashed repeatedly by.

After half an hour we reached the city of Bangkok, the most dazzling capital in the world, built on the east bank of the Menam Chao Phya. The bus made a tour of the major hotels, dropping off passengers in clusters, but Gillian and I were the only two to disembark outside the central but less palatial Embassy Hotel. I had decided to forego the more extravagant heights of hotel luxury out of consideration for Gillian's expenses.

We booked in, and after I had unpacked my suitcase and made myself presentable I returned to Gillian's room a few yards down the corridor. I knocked, but there was no response, and after a moment I opened the door and entered. Gillian stood silently by the window, staring out over the roof-tops towards the glittering spires and the blue, red and orange tiles of the distant Grand Palace and its temple complex beside the river. Her suitcase lay unopened on the bed. She was wearing the white blouse and the blue tartan mini skirt in which I had first seen her, and she looked suddenly lost and vulnerable again.

I moved quietly to join her and she didn't look round. Down on our right I saw a narrow canal leading to the river, filled with water-traffic and sampans. It was one of the *klongs* that had given Bangkok its sub-title of the Venice of the East. It made a colourful picture, but Gillian did not seem to have noticed, and after a moment I realized that she was not really looking at the distant spires either. Her eyes were misty.

"I've looked forward to this moment all my life," she said at last in a very small voice. "My father always promised to bring me here, but during the school holidays there was never enough time. He called Bangkok the most wonderful city in the East, and he said it was his second home. Daddy loved the East, he had no time for England. He said that Bangkok was worth a long stay, and that when he did bring me here we would have enough time to enjoy it."

She stopped and the mist became large tears. "Now he'll never bring me here, and I'll never enjoy it. Bangkok is a horrible city. It's all spoiled because now I have to look for his murderer!"

I knew there had to be moments like this, when her strength and determination faltered under her grief. I rested my hand on her shoulder and said softly.

"The circumstances are blacker than you ever expected, Miss Sanders, but don't let them spoil Bangkok. The city is still as wonderful as your father promised that it would be, and I'm sure that eventually you will be able to enjoy it."

She turned, and lifted her face to look at me. Then tried to blink away the tears.

"Mister Chan, isn't it — isn't it time that you stopped calling me Miss Sanders. It's too formal."

I smiled. "What would you like me to call you?"

"Not Miss Sanders. Jilly — " The tears almost came back. "No, not Jilly. My father always called me that, and I don't think I could bear it from anyone else. It will have to be Gillian. Everyone calls me Gillian."

"Allright, Gillian, no more Miss Sanders, that's a promise."

"Thank you, David." She looked suddenly embarrassed. "I can call you David, can't I? I mean, if you're going to stop calling me Miss Sanders, then it's silly for me to keep on calling you Mister Chan!"

I nodded and smiled.

She put her arms round me very suddenly and held me tight. Her heart was beating violently and her body trembled.

"David," she said in a strangled voice. "You will take care of me, won't you?"

I looked down into her wide and pleading blue eyes, and then gently stroked back the short fringe of her blonde hair. "I'll take care of you," I said, and then I leaned forward and softly kissed her waiting lips.

It was intended to be a brief kiss, just a reassurance, but her mouth responded fiercely and she clung on to me more tightly than before. There was more inside her young breast than mere loneliness and uncertainty, and she was caught up in the hot tangle of her own emotions. I realized then that Gillian Sanders was many things, a child who still needed her father, and a young woman who also needed her first lover. I remembered Belinda's warning, and wondered what else she might be, and what else she might need.

6

DAWN was the prescribed time to visit the famous floating market of Bangkok, and so at first light Gillian and I went down to the landing stages along the Menam Chao Phya. There was a vast assortment of transport, from fast narrow speedboats to large canopied launches capable of taking a score of tourists on a single cruise. I didn't want a horde of camera-draped fellow-passengers, or a rushed round trip, so I settled for a small motor launch which I hired by the hour. Our boatman was a cheerful Thai youth who wore shorts, an American baseball cap, and a tee shirt with Detroit Eagles plastered all over it. Bangkok was a favourite liberty port with American servicemen, and I guessed that our boatman had a friendly sister.

The boat pushed out on to the wide grey bosom of the Chao Phya. To our left scarlet and pink threads laced the edges of the early morning cloud banners behind the soaring spires of the city temples, while on the approaching right bank rose the great ascending tower of the Temple of the Dawn. The tower was richly decorated with bright fragments of Chinese pottery, and ringed with gods and demons, all reflecting back the brilliant dawn sun. It was flanked at each corner by four smaller towers, and each tower was surmounted by the golden trident symbol of Shiva.

"It's beautiful," Gillian said softly.

"We'll ask the boatman to stop on the way back," I promised her.

Our launch cruised slowly past the temple, the boatman smiling proudly and sharing in our pleasure. Then he turned the boat past the temple, leaving the main river and Bangkok behind, and following the course of a narrow *klong* that wound away from the city. Here the waterway was lined with wooden shacks, all raised on stilt legs and holding back a waving green skyline of coconut palms and lush green foliage that seemed to be striving to push all the ramshackle buildings into the cool brown water. I reflected that it was rather like cruising up the main street of a flooded shanty town, where laden canoes and sampans plied busily back and forth, and children swam and played with heads bobbing like sleek, butterscotch seals.

Gillian watched entranced as the picturesque river scenes floated by. We cruised beneath rickety wooden bridges that seemed on the point of collapse, and at regular intervals there would be cool, green-shaded lanes of winding water leading off from the main channel and vanishing into silent mystery. In fact I believe that for a few moments Gillian almost forgot the purpose of our visit. The floating markets attracted thousands of visitors every year, and so a number of Bangkok's leading silk and handicrafts emporiums had established themselves along the river bank. I resisted the efforts of our boatman who wanted to tie us up at the landing stages of the first two or three such places that we passed, but finally gave way with good grace when he pointed hopefully to the approaching jetty that was clearly marked with the words *Siam Anqituities*.

The boatman smiled happily, convinced that he had hopes of earning some commission after all, and lost no time in shutting down the engine and mooring his launch neatly to the jetty. Then he politely helped Gillian to step ashore.

I followed, and Gillian turned to look back at me. She was suddenly nervous and I rested my hand on her shoulder and gave her a reassuring squeeze. She smiled faintly.

Siam Antiquities consisted of a large, open-plan tourist centre, with an adjoining silk factory where pretty Thai girls weaved brightly coloured rolls of silk on their old-fashioned wooden looms. Watching the girls at work was all part of the tourist attraction, and the completed silks were on prominent display. There was also a wide range of Thai handicrafts, especially the carved wooden elephants dancers and demons, forest animals and celestial serpents, that had all become familiar at the two branches of *Exotic Art*. Gillian and I browsed briefly, and at the rear of the store found another focal point for the tourist cameras — a small, black bear chained in a circular pit. There was no shade, and by now the powerful sun was climbing high. The bear looked hot and helpless, its brown eyes dulled of any natural light.

"Poor thing," Gillian said, angrily, and loud enough to embarrass a nearby tourist fiddling anxiously with his light meter.

I nodded agreement and drew her away. Already I had decided that I was not going to find Mister Srivaji a particularly pleasant sort of person.

After a few more minutes of casual

inspection I decided that it was time to get down to business and locate the owner. We approached one of the girl assistants behind a range of sparkling gem stones, and the girl promptly hurried off to find her employer. She returned a few moments later to lead us to a small private office to one side of the centre. Inside a prosperous-looking Thai gentleman with a pre-fixed smile rose behind a large desk to greet us. He wore a spotless white suit and shirt, polished black shoes, and one of his own elegant silk ties. He was, I judged, in his mid-fifties, his thick, bristly hair prematurely grey, and his smooth face as round as a benevolent moon. His voice was cultured and well-educated, his English perfect.

"Good morning, sir — and madame — My name is Mister Srivaji. I am the owner of *Siam Antiquities*."

"I am David Chan," I said quietly. "And may I introduce to you Miss Gillian Sanders."

Srivaji's hand had been politely

extended towards me, but now it froze in mid-movement. He stared at my face, which I kept bland and inscutable in the approved Chinese fashion, and then he turned to stare at Gillian.

"Yes," he said at last. "You have the blue English eyes, and the shape of your chin is the same. You must be the daughter of my old friend."

"Mark Sanders was my father," Gillian said quietly.

"Of course," Srivaji positively beamcd. "I have seen photographs of you as a little girl, in your school uniform. Mark promised that he would bring you to visit me when next we had business together. But — " He paused. "Where is your father?"

Gillian couldn't answer, and I had to do it for her.

"Mark Sanders is dead," I informed Srivaji flatly. "He was attacked and stabbed at his home in Hong Kong five days ago."

The Thai was shocked, and if I had

not seen the chained bear that gave the lie to the warm benevolence of his round face, I would not have believed that anyone could act so well. He sat down slowly and his cheeks trembled and turned pale.

"This is not true," he said in a low whisper, and looked to Gillian for confirmation.

"It's true." Gillian bowed her head and bit her lip.

Srivaji sat in silence for a moment, he stared at her, and then at me, and finally back to Gillian again. At last he stood up and came round the desk to rest a plump hand on her arm. They were the same height, about five feet four inches, and his eyes blinked rapidly as he tried to meet her lowered gaze.

"My poor girl. I am so sorry. What can I say?" He looked flustered and ill-at-ease, and because she didn't respond he once more turned his eyes towards me.

"Mark Sanders and I were friends,"

he explained. "Very good friends. No — more than friends — we were partners in business together."

"Perhaps you can tell us about your business relationship with Gillian's father," I suggested.

"Of course, but first, please sit down."

Srivaji pulled up two chairs, dusted them and fussed around with some agitation until we were seated. Then he rang the small brass bell that rested on his desk. One of his pretty girl assistants appeared promptly and he sent her to fetch tea for the three of us. Then at last he reached his own seat, and his old habit of looking from one face to another as he clasped his hands earnestly together.

"Perhaps it is best if I start right from the beginning." He spoke uncertainly and I nodded to encourage him. He concentrated his attention on Gillian. "I first met your father ten, twelve, perhaps fifteen years ago. I forget exactly. Your mother was alive then, a most charming and gracious lady, and you were only a very small girl. You would not remember me." He paused. "Mark — I mean your father — wanted to set up a small business in Hong Kong. He had some capital left to him by his own father, and he had an interest in antiques. I had only a small shop then, in Charoen Krung Road in Bangkok. Mark visited my shop as he had visited hundreds of similar shops in South East Asia, he was looking for ideas, seeking knowledge about the different art styles and crafts, and looking for possible sources of supply."

The door opened and the girl assistant came in with a silver tray, a silver teapot, and delicate cups of silver-blue Chinese porcelain. She set the tray on the desk, poured tea into the cups, offered them round, and then bowed her way out with a graceful smile. Srivaji urged us to sip tea, and then continued:

"Mark Sanders and I took a liking

to each other. We formed a mutual respect. I invited him to my home, and eventually I offered him a proposition, which after some thought he decided to accept. The proposition was that we should become business partners in his venture in Hong Kong. He agreed to find and purchase suitable premises, while for my part I was initially to supply all his stock of antiques. It was an arrangement that enabled Mark to set up his business on a much larger scale than he had originally intended, and it was to my ultimate benefit also."

Srivaji stopped and raised his silver-blue cup briefly to his lips. Then he saw that I was not drinking and again waved an earnest hand.

"Please, do me the honour — or perhaps you prefer something stronger. I have whisky?"

"No thank you," I assured him. "Please finish your story."

He shrugged. "There is not much more to tell. Over the years the tourist trade has increased, both here and in Hong Kong, and we have both prospered. Mark quickly established his first branch of *Exotic Art* in Victoria. At first he sold mostly the Thai handicrafts that I supplied, but eventually he was able to purchase a great many rare pieces of Chinese origin. Many people escaping from Communist China brought their family heirlooms into Hong Kong, and later had to sell them. Mark sent many of those choice pieces here to Bangkok. I continued to send a rich variety of Thai handicrafts to Hong Kong. Soon Mark was able to open a second branch of *Exotic Art* in Kowloon, and I was able to transfer *Siam Antiques* to this very profitable location on the riverside."

He stopped and gazed sadly at his half empty cup.

"Now you tell me that my old friend Mark Sanders is dead. This is sudden — so unbelievable." He looked up. "Attacked and stabbed, I believe you said. Please tell me why this should happen?"

"As yet we don't know," I said, adopting my inscrutable expression once again.

"But you believe that the answers may be here in Bangkok?" His eyes were momentarily shrewd.

I nodded. "A man was disturbed at the scene of the crime. He fled, and all that we know about him is that he was almost certainly a Thai."

"I see. Are you a policeman, Mister — "

"Chan," I reminded him. "No, I'm not a policeman. I'm a private detective. Miss Sanders has engaged me to try and clear up this mystery."

"I see," Srivaji said again. "And you thought — " Again he checked the words carefully.

"We thought that perhaps you could help," I said tactfully. "After all, you were the dead man's business associate, and his friend. You must know more about his contacts in Thailand than anyone."

Srivaji nodded slowly. "That is true.

Mark came often to Bangkok, but always his trips were connected with our joint business concerns, which I have explained. Of course he enjoyed himself at the same time, but mostly in my company, and as far as I know he made no friends outside the circle of my own friends, to whom I naturally introduced him. In fact I cannot think of anything I could tell you that might help you. This news is a complete shock to me. I cannot understand it."

He stood up and came round to the front of the desk for the second time, his plump hand reaching tentatively for Gillian's shoulder.

"My poor girl, this is so terrible for you. I do not know what to do. I do not know what to say. I can only offer you my deepest sympathy. Your father was like a brother to me. If I can help you in any way you must let me know. Please do not hesitate."

While he showered her with mournful condolences I decided that some crude shock tactics might produce some interesting results. I reached for Gillian's shoulder bag which she had rested on the floor, opened it without Srivaji noticing, and withdrew the jade Buddha which I placed silently on his desk.

"Mister Srivaji." I interrupted him with a carefully controlled lack of expression. "This carving is the probable cause of your friend's death. Have you ever seen it before?"

Srivaji turned and stared at the placid smile of the green jade Buddha. His moon face registered a brief moment of confusion that was instantly blotted out by a blank mask that matched my own. He went back to his seat and reached out both hands for the image. As he touched it his hands trembled, and he lifted it with care.

"This is a wonderful piece," he said at last, and reluctantly he leaned over the desk and replaced it in front of me. "But I have not seen it before. How can you say it is responsible for Mark's murder?"

"The man who ran away from the villa was trying to steal it. He dropped it as he made his escape." I paused and regarded him closely. "It obviously comes from Thailand. Are you sure that it could not be part of one of your consignments?"

He nodded his head very firmly. "I am sure."

"But surely you do not personally vet every item in every shipment that you send to Hong Kong."

"A piece as valuable as this I would have vetted," he said positively. "This Buddha is very old, Mister Chan. It is a style we have adopted, but this particular image is older than Siam itself. Our Kingdom was founded seven hundred years ago, but this image was carved two or even three hundred years before that, probably in India. Mark Sanders did not acquire this image through me, Mister Chan, for if I had been the person fortunate enough to have found it, I would never have let it go."

I nodded slowly. "I can understand that. But we feel that more recently it must have come from Thailand. Did Sanders have any other supply sources in Bangkok?"

Srivaji shrugged. "Mark had no need of other sources, but at the same time there was nothing to stop him from buying any particular piece he fancied from any source. All dealers will buy from each other if they feel that they can pass on the item to a customer at a profit!"

We were silent, each of us revealing nothing, and finally I picked up the jade Buddha and returned it to Gillian's bag.

"Then you cannot help us?" I said.

"I do not know how to help you." He spread his hands regretfully. "I am out of my depth." He paused. "What will you do now?"

"We shall stay in Bangkok for a few days. If I fail to find any other leads then we shall have to return to Hong Kong." I hesitated delicately. "Sanders must have known other people in Bangkok whom I could approach. Perhaps if we gave you time to think you could remember a name, or something helpful."

"But of course," he was almost eager. "I would not dream of letting you take Miss Gillian away from Bangkok without visiting me again. Please come any time."

"Tomorrow," I suggested.

"Any time," he repeated. "Any time at all." He stood up and gave me an engraved card. "Here are my telephone numbers, my business and my home. If I can advise you in any way, please call."

It was hard to believe that he was anything but sincere in his desire to help, and even after thanking him it took us five minutes to escape from his profuse gestures of cordiality.

It was a pity that I could not forget the dulled brown eyes of a small black bear.

7

"**D**AVID," Gillian said doubtfully as we emerged into the blinding sunlight. "Do you really think it was a good idea to let Srivaji see the jade Buddha?"

I smiled at her. "There's an ancient Chinese proverb — when the hunter cannot find the quarry, then the hunter must become the bait in his own trap."

Gillian blinked. "I'm not sure that I understand."

"We don't know who murdered your father," I explained. "But we do know that the man who ran away from the villa was after the jade Buddha."

She understood. "Isn't that a dangerous game to play?"

"It's all part of the Chan personal service," I assured her.

We reached the landing stage where

our young friend with the baseball cap was waiting with the launch. He flashed us a wide smile as we came aboard, and promptly started the engine with one deft pull of the cord. As he unslipped his mooring line he said cheerfully.

"Floating markets now."

It was a promise more than a question, and although we had already achieved our purpose in coming here I made no objection. Gillian had been fascinated by all the colour and movement of the crowded waterways, and I felt that after the strain of the past few days she needed every moment of relaxation I could give her. I nodded and our boatman confidently turned the bows of the launch away from the jetty.

Already we were entering the riverfront village that set the bustling scene for the floating markets. Here scores of narrow, deftly-paddled canoes were shooting back and forth, all of them loaded almost to the point of sinking with an endless variety of fruit and vegetables brought from the outlying villages along the network of green water lanes. The water gypsies were almost buried under the baskets of red tomatoes, white cauliflowers and heaps of yellow pineapples. Beneath the distinctive wide straw hats the flat Thai faces all seemed to wear a smile.

Our launch manoeuvred slowly to pick a path through the swarms of water craft, and I watched the happy faces going by. Smiling girls under bright blue and orange sun-shades offered us slices of juicy red melon, or bunches of ripe, fat wax-yellow bananas. A tourist launch cruised past, and then a floating soup kitchen with an old lady tending hot bowls of rice and noodles. I watched Gillian's enraptured face, glad that she could forget her troubles if only for a few moments, and then I looked back at the happy faces drifting all around us. An unladen canoe went past, paddled lazily by a young man wearing the inevitable loose shorts and vest. His back was towards me, and his face was hidden by one of the large lampshade hats made out of yellowed palm fronds. There was something familiar about that lithe figure with the hard young muscles and the easy, almost effortless style of movement, and I found myself staring hard.

There was no hope of seeing his face unless he turned round towards me, but the sense of recognition was so strong that I raised my voice and shouted sharply:

"Hey you!"

The call startled everyone within hearing. Gillian stared up at me and our boatman's head twisted round. A dozen other faces glanced swiftly in my direction, and among them was the young man in the unladen canoe. My instinct had been right, for the smooth, handsome young face was that of the young Thai I had fought on the mountain slope behind Mark Sander's villa in Hong Kong.

As our eyes met he recognized me in turn. Alarm flooded over his face, and then he swung away and dug his paddle deep. I saw his shoulder muscles ripple and contract beneath his ragged vest, and then the canoe was accelerating away in haste.

"I wish to speak to the man in that canoe." I grabbed our boatman by the arm and snapped the words at him as I pointed out my quarry. "I will pay you twenty American dollars if you can catch him."

The boatman was eager to try. He shoved open the throttle on the outboard, and as the motor roared the launch leapt forward. There were howls of indignant complaint from the massed boats surrounding us, and more than one fist was shaken violently as a laden boat was swamped by our wake. One of the smiling girls shrieked as we narrowly missed a collision, and our boatman had to curb his sudden enthusiasm and cut down his speed. Ahead the fugitive canoe was weaving arrow-fast through the maze of traffic, and in the confusion his slender craft was pulling ahead of our clumsy launch.

I swore briefly, and our boatman saw his twenty dollars receding. He made another effort and the launch surged forward with another twist of the throttle. Our bows clipped a canoe that was piled high with melons like a mound of dark green cannon balls in the prow. The owner howled in anger as his craft was knocked aside and his melons tumbled into the river. Our boatman was by now highly flustered, but he made one last effort. The fugitive had turned into a side stream that flowed beneath one of the ramshackle wooden footbridges. Our launch banked steeply to follow, the wave created more havoc, and then abruptly the startled old lady with the floating soup kitchen was drifting slowly across our bows. She had no hope of paddling clear, and simply threw her gnarled hands up in front of her eyes and screamed a prayer. Our boatman changed course in a desperate, panic-stricken swerve, and the launch crashed to a violent stop against the wooden piles of the footbridge.

It was time to abandon the launch, and even as it slammed to a halt I was leaping from up the shuddering deck. I caught the wooden handrail of the bridge, heaved, and swung my body over to drop down neatly on the rough boards of the bridge itself. I kept moving without a pause, running over the bridge, down the crude wooden steps three at a time, and then in a fast sprint along the board walk beside the canal.

Startled faces peered at me from the open interiors of the riverside shops. A woman scooped up a naked baby and fled. I jumped over a pile of large clay water jars, and then abruptly the shops and the board walk came to an end. The river stretched before me and thirty yards away the bowed back of my quarry was still hunched over his paddle as he sped for safety. I glanced down at my feet and saw a flight of three wooden steps going down to the water level. Another canoe, half laden with sugar cane but with no human occupant, was moored there and rocking gently. I scrambled quickly aboard, cast off the line and grabbed up the paddle.

I heard more furious cries joining the general pandemonium behind me, but I did not look back. It sounded as though the entire population of the floating market was baying for my blood, having no doubt cast me as both a madman and a thief, but all that I could sort out later. I bowed my back, dug in the paddle, and concentrated on trying to overhaul the canoe in front.

He was disappearing fast up a tunnel of green gloom, where the serrated fronds of the overhanging palms and foliage almost shut out the vivid blue of the sky. The waterfront village and market vanished behind us, and suddenly we had this narrow lane of water to ourselves. I could have wished for the launch with its outboard motor, but now it was too late.

I paddled with all my strength, but the gap between myself and the lead canoe failed to narrow. However, the mystery man was paddling just as furiously, and the gap between us failed to extend. Again I had the feeling that I was competing against an equal, for although I had taken up my paddle at a later stage of the race, I had the cargo of sugar cane to slow me down. I was tempted to heave the long green bundles of cane overboard, but that would have meant resting my paddle and losing speed for a few vital seconds. I felt that I couldn't afford to lose even one stroke of the paddle, and so I kept going. My arms and back muscles began to ache, and I could only hope that my quarry was also feeling the strain.

I heard shouts from behind, and risked a brief glance over my shoulder. Two more canoes had taken up the pursuit, but I guessed that it was me they were calling upon to stop. In their eyes I was the mad thief who had stolen a load of sugar cane from one of their friends.

For five minutes the unrelenting race continued, round bend after bend of the twisting tunnel of water. The two men behind had stopped shouting and we all paddled in grim silence. The young Thai from the villa looked back occasionally and redoubled his efforts, but each extra spurt from him only prompted an extra spurt from me. It seemed that despite every effort either of us could make we were connected by an invisible tow bar and the distance between the two canoes could not be altered. I began to sweat, not a Chinese discomfort but I am half English, and my back felt as though it must break.

The race ended as abruptly as it had begun. The young Thai either tired of it, or decided that it had no future. Without warning he leaned heavily to one side, and then hooked his paddle in a wide sweep that brought his canoe head round to spear directly at the left bank. He had aimed for a gap in the foliage, and suddenly he was lost from sight.

I plunged my paddle deep in a series of fast, closing strokes, and then made the same manoeuvre in my turn. I ducked my head to shoot under the slanting bole of a palm tree that overhung the river, and then my canoe was bumping violently to a stop beside the now empty canoe of my quarry. The only clue to his line of flight lay in the rustling of the leaves and branches that had closed behind him.

I pulled myself up by the trunk of the palm tree and jumped ashore. The foliage parted under my weight and I continued the pursuit through a green tangle laced with the exotic red blooms of wild orchids. I heard a faint crashing ahead of me and plunged in that general direction, but here the trees and the undergrowth were so thick that I was quickly lost. I emerged after a few minutes in a small clearing and stopped to listen for my bearings.

I could hear two clumsy forms crashing

through the undergrowth behind me, and I cursed because the noise they were making would blot out any further faint rustles from the young Thai who was making good his silent escape. I hesitated, hoping for a whisper of sound that I might be able to pinpoint as coming from my elusive fugitive, but then the two men who had followed me from the floating market burst into the clearing. They let out exultant yells, and rushed up from either side to grab at my arms.

I could have hurled them aside with the appropriate judo throws, but by now there was very little point. I had already lost my man, and even if I had reacted violently to break free it would be hopeless to try and find him again. The two agitated boatmen would only continue shouting and blundering about in my wake. Also they believed passionately that they were in the right, and I already had enough to explain without adding injury to insult. I relaxed, cursing inwardly, and allowed them to restrain me.

They were two small but wiry and determined little men wearing grey shorts and blue cotton shirts. While holding on to me with one hand they each gesticulated excitedly with the other, at the same time talking rapidly. They spoke neither English nor Chinese, and I spoke no Thai, and so there were a few moments of heated spluttering. I placated them with smiles, and finally by the more practical expedient of producing my wallet and offering each of them a ten dollar bill. The older man was briefly indignant with the thought I should consider him bribable and corruptible, but when he saw that I had no objection to returning to the market with them he became more compliant.

I let them lead me back to the canoes, and then we began a less hectic journey back to the main river. I again paddled the borrowed canoe laden with sugar cane, while my two self-appointed jailers kept a watchful pace one on either side.

The palm fronds finally parted above our heads. The riverfront shops appeared, and the wooden footbridge with the main area of the floating market beyond. A crowd had gathered on the board walk to give a voluble welcome as I tied my canoe back in its place at the bottom of the wooden steps. I climbed ashore, and straight into another torrent of indignation from a spirited old woman who awaited me, I guessed that the boat I had used was her property, and so I smiled hopefully and again produced my wallet. At the same moment I saw Gillian, and our own boatman with the baseball cap and the Detroit Eagles tee shirt on the fringe of the crowd. I called them over and with the young Thai's help managed to translate my apologies and my assurances that I was not a common thief of unguarded canoes.

The pacification process took another ten minutes. The old grandmother finally accepted twenty dollars for the use of her boat and the calming of her ruffled feelings. Then there was the soup kitchen woman, whose feelings were also ruffled and in a state of shock, and the boatman whose melons had been knocked overboard during the confusion before I had abandoned the launch. Ten dollars apiece settled their complaints, and suddenly all the round moon faces were cheerful again. After all, nobody had really been hurt, and some people had made money. It all became a huge joke.

When we were able to return to the launch I had one final piece of explaining to do. Gillian was still in a state of bewilderment over my incomprehensible actions.

"The man in the canoe was the same man who ran away from your father's villa on The Peak," I told her regretfully. "I seem to be fated to lose him immediately every time I set eyes on him."

"Then we were right to come to Bangkok," Gillian said in a voice that was half elation and half anxiety. "We are on the right trail."

I nodded soberly, and steadied her as the launch began to move out into the river on its return journey.

"What will you do next?" Gillian demanded.

I glanced at my watch. "By now Belinda and Tracey should be landing at Don Muang Airport. By the time we get back to the hotel they will have arrived. I think we should join them for lunch."

8

WHEN we returned to the Embassy Hotel it was noon, and Belinda and Tracey had already established themselves at the bar with pre-luncheon gins and tonic. Belinda wore a short, slim dress of peacock blue, while Tracey favoured crisp white slacks and a lime green blouse that set off her flame red hair. They both looked cool and adorable as always, two perfect female forms that a man might hesitate to approach, preferring to admire from afar in case a closer inspection might reveal some disappointing flaw in voice or personality. There were at least six pairs of male eyes doing just that, but I knew that there were no flaws in their perfection, and joined my two visions of beauty with no qualms.

"Hi," they said together.

"Hi," I answered equably. "How was your flight?"

"Very smooth," Belinda said. "I didn't feel a single bump, How have you been getting along?"

Our conversation would not have been very private with the four of us spread out along bar stools, so I suggested that we adjourn to a table. Before doing so I refreshed their glasses, and ordered a tall iced beer for myself. Gillian decided that she too would try a gin and tonic. When we were all comfortably seated I recounted the events of the morning.

Belinda and Tracey listened with close interest until I had finished, and then Tracey said seriously,

"David, are you sure that it was the same man?"

"I couldn't be mistaken," I said. "I fought him face to face on the mountain, and when I called out to him this morning he looked directly into my face again. It was the same man."

"But what would he be doing in the floating market? Obviously he isn't a tourist soaking up the local colour, and equally obviously he couldn't be just another farmer from one of the outlying villages."

I smiled at her. "While we're spelling out the obvious, it's equally certain that he isn't just an ordinary sneak thief. The very fact that he's reappeared here proves that. Ordinary sneak thieves simply do not operate on an international basis. They don't jet from one capital to another."

"So we can positively dismiss the theory that Sanders could have been killed by a casual burglar," Belinda mused aloud. "That means that there must be something more significant behind his death. David, do you still think that there may be some involvement with one of the big art smuggling rackets?"

"It's the strongest possibility," I said. "The whole background to this case is one of art treasures and antiques.

And Thailand is a country with a rich cultural heritage where such objects could be plundered."

"Speculation is no basis for investigation," Tracey warned me, repeating an old rule that she had learned with the F.B.I.

"Very true," I agreed, "But until we have some proven facts it will have to suffice. A blind man can only feel in the dark, and trust to his natural instincts."

"Another ancient Chinese proverb," Tracey told Gillian disparagingly. "He makes them up as he goes along."

"We do have one proven fact." Belinda was always the practical one. "The man who ran away from the villa in Hong Kong and here in Bangkok. And David did spot him only a few hundred yards away from *Siam Antiquities* — perhaps his business was there and not in the floating market."

I smiled my approval, because she had neatly clarified the most important point. Those splendid hazel eyes regarded me calmly from behind the golden butterfly spectacles, and she concluded:

"What are our next moves, David?"

"I think that tomorrow Gillian and I will make a return visit to *Siam Antiquities*. We promised Mister Srivaji that we would see him again, and also I should like to see his face when I tell him that the man we suspect of murdering his old friend and business partner was lurking dangerously close to his own back door."

"And what about Traccy and I?"

"I suggest that you work separately, and assume the same role that almost tempted Mister Wang in Kowloon." I paused. "In fact, it might be better to improve on that story slightly. You won't be representing a private collector, but instead a small private museum. You can hint that you have a free hand to purchase exhibits of any kind, the only criterion being that they must be rare and genuine."

Belinda nodded wisely. "It's a good approach. The demand for real antiquities is now too great for them all to be supplied by legitimate means. That's why the looting and the smuggling rackets have become big business, and most of the buyers do use intermediary agents. By letting a middleman handle the transactions the real buyers can salve their consciences and pretend that they don't really know how the pieces were acquired. It also helps to protect them from any subsequent police action if it can be proved that the pieces were stolen, although that very rarely happens."

"When do we start?" Tracey asked.

"Right after luncheon," I suggested. "It might not be a good idea to go directly to Srivaji, he has reasons for being wary. So I think you'll have to waste some time this afternoon in making some general calls on the other art shops in Bangkok. Tomorrow morning will be soon enough to take a boat out to *Siam Antiquities*, and if Srivaji does then decide to check back on your movements we can hope that he'll believe that he hasn't been singled out for any special attention."

Belinda nodded agreement. "An all round tour would make our role look right. But when will you go back to *Siam Antiquities?*"

"Later tomorrow," I answered. "I don't want to harass Srivaji too much before you arrive. I'd prefer him to feel as free as possible to carry on his normal routine. I won't try any more shock tactics with him until after you've paid your call."

"So what do you intend to do this afternoon?" Tracey enquired as though she knew the answer.

"I think I'll show Gillian the sights," I replied.

Tracey looked helplessly at Belinda. "Hong Kong or Bangkok, it's all the same," she said. "We work, while he plays."

"But it's going to cost him," Belinda cheered her. "We need at least two more gins and tonic, and I'm very hungry."

★ ★ ★

The following morning I gave Belinda and Tracey an hours start before Gillian and I again went down to the tourist landing stages beside the Menam Chao Phya. The sun was already high, promising another scorching hot day beneath flawless blue skies, and all the regular excursion launches had long departed. However, I soon spotted a familiar baseball cap and the *Detroit Eagles* tee shirt. No one had hired our young friend with his small private motor launch, and so he was happy to oblige us again. We had caused him some awkward moments yesterday, but he was a cheerful soul and I am confident that he found me generous enough.

We set off again, turning past that magnificent porcelain tower of the Temple of the Dawn. The branching *klong* was as busy as before, with the same endless variety of motor and muscle powered craft, and the same indefatigable swarms of plump, laughing children swimming and diving in the warm brown waters. It seemed all too soon that we were back at the silk factories and the large handicrafts emporiums, and tying up once more at the wooden landing stage beside *Siam Antiquities*.

A number of the tourist launches were still there, and so I looked among the idling crowds for Belinda and Tracey. I saw them almost immediately, for although there were a number of very attractive women in sight, my two partners were by far the most eye-catching pair of them all. It was a fact which I was not alone in appreciating, for I saw that they had found a companion.

I assumed the man to be an American, for he had the easy stance and confident grin that Americans seem to adopt the world over. He was a big, handsome man of about forty, with dark hair and a rugged charm to his weather-tanned face. He wore fawn coloured slacks and a check shirt open wide at the neck, and he twirled a pair of expensive sunglasses in one capable hand. I noted that he carried no camera, and none of the other cluttered accoutrements of a tourist, and if he was overawed by the delightful duo he had accosted he showed no sign.

All three were contributing an equal and cheerful enthusiasm to their conversation, and while I watched the American made an offer that was promptly accepted. The two girls hitched their handbags more firmly on their shoulders, and allowed the stranger to take each of them by the arm and lead them away. They walked through the colourful displays ranged around the store, and entered a small tea room on the far side. I saw them sit down at a secluded table. Belinda and Tracey were still smiling, and the American raised one hand to wave casually at a waiter.

I felt a moment of resentment at this unknown man who was making himself so immediately comfortable with my girls. I tried to analyse the feeling, and could not decide whether it was jealousy because another man was paying them such designful attention, or mere annoyance because they were being distracted from their job. Long ago I had established an easy brother-and-sisters kind of relationship with Belinda and Tracey, for I knew that any close romantic involvement with either of them would have to exclude the other, and would run the risk of breaking up a highly successful detective agency. It was a relationship which we all accepted and maintained, but at the same time it was impossible for me not to be aware that they were two exceedingly desirable young women.

However, at this stage we were supposed to be unknown to each other, and so it would be impossible to devise any reasonable excuse to interfere. Also Gillian was waiting for me with a puzzled look on her face, and I had to accept that I was hardly fit to distinguish between professional irritation and sexual jealousy in my own mind.

"Let's find Srivaji," I said.

Gillian looked up at me curiously, but refrained from reminding me that that was the purpose of our visit. I turned away from the tea room and left Belinda and Tracey and their new companion to their own devices. Only Gillian looked back, staring briefly over her shoulder.

Srivaji was in his office. He looked the same as before, but I noticed that there was a different design on his rich silk tie, and the white suit, although identical to the one he had worn yesterday, had been freshly donned this morning. He greeted us warmly.

"Mister Chan, and Miss Sanders, I am so glad that you could come back." He insisted that we be seated, and rang the small handbell again to order the inevitable tea, before he continued: "This morning I had a letter from Mister Robinson, your father's solicitor in Hong Kong. He informs me officially of your father's sad death, and also that in the absence of a will you are your father's sole beneficiary. You now own fifty percent of *Exotic Art*, Miss Sanders — which means that you and I have now become business partners."

Gillian nodded. "Mister Robinson did inform me about that."

"But of course." Srivaji paused delicately. "May I ask please if you have formed any plans or intentions concerning your inheritance?"

"Mister Robinson advised me to leave the running of the two shops to the managers in charge — at least for the time being."

Srivaji nodded gently. "That would be best. I think that both your father's managers are honest men, and Mister Wang, the senior manager at the Kowloon branch has always appeared to me to be very capable. I feel that while they and the solicitor are looking after your interests, then you need concern yourself very little with the complexities of the business. The two branches of *Exotic Art* are now well-established, and your fifty percent ownership will provide you with more than an adequate income." He smiled like a moon-faced uncle. "Naturally if there are any problems I will fly to Hong Kong immediately to help you resolve them. I hope that our future relationship in business, like that with your father before you, will always be based on a close personal friendship."

Gillian was impressed by his sincerity, and when he paused she nodded earnestly. Then the girl assistant appeared with the silver teapot and the silver-blue cups, and when we had been served and it was polite to intervene I changed the subject.

"Mister Srivaji," I pressed him gently. "Have you had time to think back as you promised, and perhaps remembered anything that could help with my investigation?"

Srivaji looked less benevolent, and more unhappy.

"I have tried," he said, "But this whole affair is still totally beyond my comprehension. Mark was a good man, and one respected because he knew the East so well. He had no enemies that I know of, and certainly none here in Bangkok. The jade Buddha you showed me explains nothing. It is a rare and priceless relic, but in the nature of our business we have both handled many such works of art. I feel, Mister Chan, that your investigation here in Bangkok is perhaps misguided." He spread his hands wide in a shrug of despair. "Your answers must remain in Hong Kong."

"I do not think so," I told him gently, "For the young Thai we are seeking in connection with Mark Sander's murder is definitely here in Bangkok. I saw him yesterday, only a few minutes after we left the building. He was in a canoe, and although I gave chase I unfortunately lost him again."

"He was here!" Srivaji looked shocked, and then disbelief took over. "But how can you be so sure it was the same man?"

"I am sure!" I left no room for doubt in my voice. "He is a young man, about thirty years old, and very handsome. Yesterday he wore shorts and a white vest, and a large lampshade hat."

"There are many young men such as this," Srivaji protested.

"This one was very fit, and very athletic," I continued. "And he's a very skilled boxer. It wouldn't surprise me to find that he's well known around the sports halls."

Srivaji looked worried. "I still do not know him. And I cannot think why he should be seen in the vicinity of my shop."

Once the shock effect had worn off there was no point in pressing the matter, and although I tried a few more questions in the hope of unsettling his composure there was nothing more to be learned. When we decided to leave Srivaji saw us off the premises with a surge of final declarations of his goodwill towards Gillian. While she nodded attentively to his remarks I glanced towards the tea rooms, hoping to spot Belinda and Tracey. They and their amiable American had departed, but as my gaze swept back across the store I noticed a point of interest that I had missed on our previous visit.

I indicated the range of polished, grey-white handicrafts shaped out of potter's clay, and asked briefly, "Are these made locally?"

Srivaji spared them a glance. "No," he said. "We import them from Chieng Mai. There are several pottery factories there."

I nodded absently, as though it was unimportant, and said no more.

★ ★ ★

When we were aboard the launch and returning to Bangkok Gillian asked me what I planned to do next. I could only shrug and offer what she obviously considered a non-aggressive and somewhat uninspiring answer.

"Our friend Srivaji is under pressure," I told her. "He knows we have the jade Buddha, and he knows we've seen the young Thai very close to his own base of operations. I think he's worried, and consequently we have to wait for him to make the next move."

"But if he is just as bewildered and uninvolved as he pretends to be, then he won't be making any moves," Gillian said doubtfully. "Then what do we do?"

"Then we have to think of another angle," I said blandly.

Gillian looked as if she failed to find any deeper satisfaction in that, but decided not to press the issue any further. Instead she stared gloomily at a long speedboat that went flashing past in a curtain of spray. The speedboat's wake set up a wave that rocked everything on the river, but when it had subsided we settled down in silence to enjoy the rest of the trip.

It was very relaxing cruising slowly down the *klong*, with the overhanging palm fronds and the close, riverfront shops and weathered wooden houses shutting out the worst heat of the sun. I closed my eyes and listened to the chug of our engine, the splashing of paddles, and the muffled cries of romping children and the ever hopeful floating pedlars. I opened them again when our outboard spluttered as the boatman closed down the throttle.

Glancing ahead I saw a traffic jam. Immediately in front of us was another launch, slightly larger than our own. Belinda and Tracey were seated in the back, and still chatting cheerily with their new male companion. They didn't acknowledge me, but that was because we were still supposed to be strangers. Beyond their launch was the cause of the delay that had enabled us to catch them up. Two long lines of floating barges had become momentarily entangled as they tried to pass each other on the narrow canal.

The boatmen on both strings were shouting with careless unconcern, running to and fro along bulwarks almost awash, and thrusting valiantly upon their long steering poles. Slowly the barges were sorted out and held apart until the string moving downstream had drifted clear. The launch ahead began to move again, seeking an opportunity to shoot past and overtake the slower barges. It was held up again because the fast speedboat was coming back.

I watched the upstream barges moving past, the barge-handlers relaxing now and drawing their poles inboard while the engine on the lead barge provided all the power. They grinned at us and Gillian waved. I could hear the speedboat racing up but I closed my eyes, waiting for the repeated rock and roll motion of its passing wave.

From the launch in front of me I suddenly heard Belinda scream:

"*David, LOOK OUT!*"

I spun round in my seat, and in the bows of the fast-approaching speedboat I saw a man crouching with a rifle in his hands. The intent to kill was in his fierce slit eyes, and the rifle was aimed at my heart.

9

THE rifle was the self-loading Armalite M 16, the basic infantry weapon used by the American forces in Vietnam. It was lightweight for easy carrying over rough terrain, and chromium-plated to resist rust in wet jungles. I knew that it was also fast and accurate. The man behind it was a Thai in late middle age, his round face unusually creased and wrinkled, and the effect heightened by its present harsh set of concentration. He wore a brightly patterned blue and green *sarong*, and a strip of gay blue silk tied in a piratical headband. His brown hands held the rifle in a capable grip, the stock pulled firmly into his shoulder.

Belinda's desperate cry was still echoing in the horrified air, and as the speedboat rushed up the man in the bows started to swivel neatly on the ball of his bare left foot and his crouching knee. I saw no more, for in the split second before he drew level I moved as fast as I have ever moved in all my life. I flung myself in a lightning rolling action along the short length of the launch, gathered up Gillian's startled, flinching body with one arm, and then plunged over the stern of the boat and into the river. Behind me the Armalite M 16 had opened fire in a lethal spray of bullets.

I heard the savage hammer of the explosions, and felt and dived deeply for the muddy bottom of the *klong*. I kept a firm grip on Gillian who struggled like a terrorstricken eel, and pulled her down under one arm.

The thick, swirling brown water reduced visibility to less than a yard. For all practical purposes I could see nothing, and the only sensations that reached me were those of sound and movement. I heard the muffled echoes of the assault rifle, the slap of more bullets hitting the surface of the water above me, and then the thunderous roaring as the speedboat swept over our heads. I felt the shock waves of its passing, the surge of sudden undercurrents, and the disturbed agitation of water all around me. My right shoulder dragged along the muddy bottom as I swam hard to escape the searching bullets, and Gillian continued to thrash in a blind frenzy in my grasp.

Her panic finally forced us to the surface. Our heads broke water and she spluttered desperately for air while I searched for the long black speedboat. It was disappearing fast upstream and mercifully showed no intentions of turning back. I changed my crushing grip on Gillian to enable her to gasp more easily for the life-giving air, and then trod water briefly as I looked round at the confusion that remained.

Our launch had crashed into the bank, and I was relieved to see that our boatman, although he had lost his smile and his baseball cap, was at least alive. He had been standing forward at the wheel, and the murderous burst of rifle fire had swept the centre and the stern of the boat in its search for my rolling body. I looked downstream and saw two heads forging strongly towards me. In the lead was Belinda, streaking along with a fast overarm crawl, while a few yards behind her the American I had yet to meet was expending as much energy but achieving less speed. Behind them Tracey was still in the second launch, directing her boatnen to circle round and pick us all up.

Belinda reached us in a flurry of spray, changing her stroke and turning deftly on to her back as she came up beside me. Her long lashes blinked water away from the soft hazel eyes that were as anguished as I had ever seen them as she asked anxiously,

"David, are you alright?"

"I'm rather wet, and my dignity is somewhat deflated." I tried to reassure her with some of the old banter, but the concern remained in her eyes.

Gillian was still coughing helplessly between us, and Belinda helped me to support her. She was badly frightened, but as far as I could see she had suffered no real injury. The American reached us while we were still trying to calm her.

"Hell," he exploded, blowing water as he came to a stop. "What was all that about?" He shook the water away from his hair, decided that he had asked the wrong question first, and added promptly: "Are you people hurt?"

"I don't think so," I said. "Our friend with the rifle missed."

The launch with Tracey commanding from the stern was edging slowly towards us, and so we made a combined effort to close the gap. Gillian still needed help, and as Belinda and I pushed her up over the side, Tracey knelt to haul her in. Tracey looked searchingly into my face, and in that moment I saw Belinda's concern mirrored for the second time in the worried eyes of emerald green. I forced my reassuring smile again to let her know that I was unharmed.

The American and I heaved ourselves up together, and then I turned to offer an unnecessary hand to Belinda. She was as nimble as the rest of us, and came over the side like some dripping goddess of the deep. She wore stockings, panties, and a short blouse plastered wetly over her briefly heaving bosom, and she looked magnificent. Beside her Venus would have returned to the sea in shame. She stood for a few seconds to catch her breath, and then she stooped to pick up and replace her spectacles. She stepped casually into her discarded skirt and zipped it up over her left hip.

"Thanks for the warning," I said quietly. "Without it I would have died, and never known what had hit me."

Belinda smiled faintly, and for once she had no words. I would have kissed her except that we had company. The

American said uncertainly,

"Say, do you folks all know each other?"

I had to thank him for his help, and Tracey reluctantly made the introductions.

"David and Gillian are friends of ours," she admitted. "Jack, this is David Chan, and Gillian Sanders — David, meet Jack Holden." She paused and her eyes conveyed a warning as she added: "Jack is a businessman who has settled out here in Thailand. He's a part-owner of *Siam Antiquities!*"

That was my second surprise for the day, but it was too late to fish for any further information. A police motor launch was coming up fast, and they obviously had questions of their own to ask.

★ ★ ★

We spent the next hour in a small, neat, riverside police station, where the red white and blue barred flag of Thailand fluttered bravely over the cool verandah. The police officers were smart and efficient in khaki uniforms with white webbing belts and snowball helmets, but only the sergeant-in-charge spoke a minimum of English. I explained to him as well as I was able to that I had no idea why my boat should have been attacked, or who the attackers might have been. The girls supported my story, and Holden showed more genuine bewilderment.

Outside the river was a buzz of feverish, police-initiated activity, but it all seemed to lead nowhere. I guessed that the police were hunting for the black speedboat, or for anyone who saw it go past and might have recognized the men aboard, but they were having no success. Boats hurried to and fro, constables came and went, and at the end of it no one seemed any wiser. My unfortunate boatman with the *Detroit Eagles* tee shirt was subjected to a stiff interrogation, for he was the only person connected with our party who spoke Thai, and I knew from the wretched looks he gave me that I would never hire his launch again. As far as he was concerned I was Trouble with a capital T.

Finally the police sergeant tired of asking the same questions and receiving the same blank answers. He made a point of noting down all our names and hotel addresses, and promised to continue his enquiries along the river. He was baffled and frustrated, but he remained polite to the last. He apologized for all the inconvenience we had suffered and allowed us to go.

The two launches took us all back to Bangkok, and there I paid off my now gloomy boatman, and added a hundred dollars to repair the angry bullet scars that riddled his launch, and to pay for a new baseball cap. He accepted the money with good grace, but he was still glad to see the back of me.

Holden parleyed briefly with Belinda and Tracey. He needed a change of clothes, but promised them that he would look them up again later. Then he called a taxi, waved a cheery farewell and disappeared into the traffic stream heading south along Maharaj Road. I called another taxi and took the girls back to the hotel.

While I cleaned up and donned fresh clothes I pondered grimly over the vicious nature of the attack that had just failed. I had not expected an enemy as ruthless as the one I undoubtedly faced, and I regretted that I had not packed the 9 millimetre Chinese automatic that reposed uselessly in the top drawer of my desk in the agency office in Hong Kong. Now it was too late, my emergency hardware was a thousand miles away, and on this case I would have to manage without it.

When I considered myself presentable I called on Gillian in her room. She had taken a hot bath and now looked an only slightly paler version of her old self in a neat, yellow-patterned dress that suited her short blonde hair. Her blue eyes still held traces of anxiety, and on impulse she hugged me and held me close. I kissed her to soothe the last of her fears away, and then we walked along the corridor to the room that Belinda and Tracey shared.

Tracey invited us in, she was sitting on the edge of one of the two single beds and carefully filing her nails. Belinda was still splashing in the shower, but she insisted that there was no need for us to wait for her, she could overhear our talk quite clearly through the half open door.

Gillian and I sat down on the second bed.

"What happened when you saw Srivaji?" I asked quietly.

Tracey frowned. "Nothing really. We spent about twenty minutes exploring *Siam Antiquities* before we approached him. We talked for a while about some of the better pieces on display, and then Belinda gave him the story that we worked out yesterday. She hinted that we were representatives for a small museum in America that was interested in buying some new exhibits. Srivaji simply didn't bite at the bait. He tried to sell us some of the pieces we had already seen, but if he had anything illegitimate under the counter, then he was keeping it well hidden."

"Do you think he might have had something under the counter?"

Tracey pursed her full red lips, a gesture of doubt that made her mouth almost irresistably kissable.

"I don't know, David. Either Srivaji is innocent, or the sudden death of his partner and your own presence here in Bangkok have made him very careful. I'd say he has second thoughts about everything, and at a time like this he's taking no chances with strange buyers."

Belinda emerged from the shower with a large towel wrapped around her.

"If Srivaji is innocent, then he's the only really innocent art dealer that I've ever met," she said bluntly. "They all have something they like to hold back from the pawing hands of the uninitiated. Even legitimate pieces are kept out of the reach of the routine bargain hunters, waiting for the right buyer with the right price."

"So Srivajl is scared," I said. "That tells us something."

"But not enough," Tracey said wryly.

"What about Jack Holden?" I asked her. "Where does he fit into the picture?"

Tracey chuckled, and showed me a teasing smile.

"I wondered how long it would take you to ask about Jack." She paused to inspect her newly manicured nails, stretched her lovely long legs to make herself more comfortable, exchanged more smiles with Belinda, and finally decided to tell me the story.

"After we left Srivaji we wandered over to the silk factory to watch the Thai girls working their looms. That was where we found Jack, or rather he found us. At first he seemed to be just an ordinary nice friendly guy, trying hard to get acquainted with a couple of good-looking girls. Then he accompanied us back into the store. He was familiar with all the salesgirls, he knew them all by name, and when we stopped to look at some jewelry he offered to make us a present of a couple of the little filigree silver brooches that caught my eye. We protested that they were too expensive to accept, and that was when he told us that they would cost him nothing because he was a part owner in the store."

There was a moment of contemplative silence while the three girls looked at me, and I didn't know who to look at in turn.

"So Srivaji has another partner," I said at last. "Yet he gave me the impression that he was the sole owner of *Siam Antiquities*. I wonder why?"

"Perhaps he thought it had no relevance," Gillian offered vaguely. "After all, I only own part of *Exotic Art*. My father had no interest in

Siam Antiquities except that he and Srivaji exchanged art works of Thai and Chinese origin. Perhaps Srivaji thought that it was none of our business that he had another partner here in Thailand."

"I'm still puzzled," I confessed. "If Holden is another partner, then what, I wonder, is his contribution to the partnership?"

Tracey shrugged. "Perhaps he just has money to invest. We did stay with him in the hope of getting some more positive information, although we were careful not to ask direct questions. He bought us tea and joined us in the trip back to Bangkok, but he didn't let anything else slip about himself. Then the man in the speedboat opened fire on your launch, and you know the rest."

I nodded grimly. Tracey fell silent, and then Belinda appeared from behind a screen, minus her towel but respectably clothed in her peacock blue dress.

"What about the man in the boat?"

Belinda asked. "Was he the man you've been chasing all over Hong Kong and Bangkok?"

I remembered that Belinda had not yet seen the young Thai from the villa. "No," I informed her. "I've never seen this man before, but I'm sure that I'll recognize him again just as easily. He was a lot older than my friend from the villa, and his face was unusually harsh and weather-beaten for a Thai."

"I think that I shall recognize him too," Belinda said grimly. "I'll never forget the way he crouched looking down the barrel of that rifle." She paused. "It was a modern-looking weapon that he used."

I nodded. "It was an American Armalite M 16, but I would imagine that they are fairly easy to acquire in this particular corner of the world. There are plenty of American forces stationed here, and we're only a couple of doors away from Vietnam."

I wasn't really interested in the rifle,

and I looked to Tracey again. "It's a pity that Holden was with you when the attack took place. He knows now that you and Belinda, and Gillian and I, are all well-acquainted. And if he is Srivaji's partner then it means that by now Srivaji will also know. The cover that you and Belinda tried to establish as a couple of independent buyers is now smashed."

"That is unfortunate," Tracey agreed. "But it works both ways. Jack Holden can now figure out the truth about us, but in turn we have also learned something about him."

"But not enough," I said. "I want to know more."

"He promised to see us again," Belinda reminded me cheerfully. "He knows that we are staying at this hotel, so I wouldn't be surprised if he appears here later this evening. You may get the opportunity to pump him then."

* * *

An hour later I was fastening a neat knot in my neck-tie in my own room, preparing to join the girls again for dinner, and still thinking about Jack Holden. The American's role in this business intrigued me, and I wondered if by now he was in close conference with Srivaji. If so he would probably be smart enough to volunteer all the explanations and information I needed the next time we met, and my task then would be to determine what was fact and what was fiction. I was still contemplating that coming conversation when I heard a brisk knock on my door.

With Holden on my mind I was half prepared to find him waiting in the corridor when I answered that knock. Instead I found a smooth Thai face with a disconcerting shrewdness in the sharp brown eyes. He was a few inches taller than the average among his countrymen, and his shoulders were held square in the manner of a man accustomed to self-discipline. He wore a peaked cap, and the spotlessly smart uniform of a senior police officer. He said with a smile.

"Good evening, Mister Chan. I am Inspector Karachorn of the Bangkok Police."

10

I TRIED to match the bland smile of my visitor, and stood aside to make him welcome.

"This is an unexpected honour, Inspector. Please come in."

He removed his cap as he came through the door, and tucked it neatly under his arm in the manner of efficient policemen the world over. He was relaxed as he faced me, yet his shoulders remained square. His eyes revealed a mind that never fully slept, and his smile remained.

"Unexpected, Mister Chan — surely not? Surely you did not think that we would allow a visitor to our country to be attacked in bright daylight in a crowded tourist area without the most thorough investigation. This is a most serious matter!"

I nodded soberly, for I should have

known that the business couldn't end with a mere hour at a riverside police station.

"Forgive me, Inspector, I meant no slight on the Bangkok Police." I paused and then asked. "Does this visit mean that you have found the speedboat, and the men who attacked me?"

"We have found the speedboat," he admitted calmly. "It was tied up at an isolated landing stage along one of the minor *klongs*. The man who owned the speedboat was found in an empty boathouse nearby. He was very neatly tied up with rope, his mouth was gagged, and his eyes were blindfolded with a strip of dirty sacking. He was very frightened. He told us that he was attacked from behind, and that some persons unknown stole his speedboat. Later the speedboat was returned — after it had been used for the attack upon your launch."

"And the men who made that attack?"

Karachorn shrugged sadly. "We can

find no trace of them. The man who owned the speedboat saw no faces. That is why our enquiry must return to you."

"But I am at a loss to help you," I said regretfully. "I don't know who those men were, or why they should attempt to murder me. I gave a description of the man who fired the rifle to the sergeant at the police station by the river, but the man at the wheel of the speedboat I did not see. I have told the police all that I know."

"I must apologize, Mister Chan, but I do not think so." Karachorn spoke with equal regret. He regarded me gravely for a moment, and then said, "Mister Chan, you have a Chinese name, but I believe that one of your parents was English. I am a Thai, but like most of my people I have been exposed to the brash pretence of a multitude of Americans visiting my country. It would seem that both of us have been influenced by the crude manners of the West, and so perhaps we can dispense with some of the traditional Asian politeness and come more directly to the point. This morning I received a long cable from your own police force in Hong Kong — to be more precise it was from a Detective Chief Superintendent Davies!"

I realized that I had been fencing with a man who was not only intelligent, but also well informed. I smiled to concede that he had scored a point.

"Please go on," I said.

"Your Superintendent Davies is currently investigating a murder in Hong Kong," Karachorn continued blandly. "The dead man was an art dealer who made frequent visits to Bangkok, and who also had a business partnership with a Mister Srivaji who owns *Siam Antiquities* in the floating market area. Basically the cable was a formal request for all the information we can provide on the dead man's trips to Bangkok, and also on the partner, Mister Srivaji. It was mentioned incidentally that the David

Chan Detective Agency was involved with the case, and that you, and your two lady assistants, were operating in Bangkok on behalf of the murdered man's daughter."

I nodded in total agreement and said wryly, "It would seem that Superintendent Davies has told you everything there is to know."

"Please," Karachorn begged, "Do not feel any animosity towards your police friend in Hong Kong. He needs information, and one day perhaps I will need information from him. Police co-operation between different national forces has to work both ways, and it has to be complete."

"There is no animosity," I assured him. "It is always my policy to co-operate as closely as possible with the police."

He smiled approval. "Then perhaps you can share with me the results of your investigations?"

"Willingly," I said. "But so far I have no results to share. I know that my presence here is unwelcome, and that some persons unknown obviously consider me a real danger. But I am still only hunting for clues. I have found nothing."

"You found a man in the floating markets," Karachorn corrected me gently. "Yesterday you caused a great disturbance by pursuing a man in a canoe!"

"But I failed to catch him. I thought that I recognized his face, but I could not get close enough to be sure. I could have been mistaken."

"From where did you think his face might be familiar?"

I could not withhold the information, and Davies had probably included it in his cable anyway, so I told him about the young Thai who had fled from Mark Sander's villa in Hong Kong. Karachorn listened thoughtfully, and remained pensive afterwards. It seemed that our interview might become a long one, and so I offered him a drink.

"No thank you," he waved the

whisky bottle away. "I do not touch alcohol." Then to prove that he was not unfriendly he added, "However, I will sit down."

We both found seats, and he laid his cap carefully on the edge of the bed. He faced me with his hands resting on his knees, and his bright brown eyes gazing intently into my own.

"Mister Chan, you claim that so far your investigation has produced no facts, but it is clear to me that you do have suspicions. The two very beautiful ladies who assist you have been circulating around the Bangkok art shops, pretending to be private buyers for an American museum. That to me is significant."

He stopped, but when I did not respond he began again.

"We both know that for a large number of rich private collectors and for even larger number of small town museums in Europe and America, the possession of a display of rare art relics

172

has become a symbol of prestige. The poor countries that have given birth to splendid ages of culture in the past are now being robbed of their own cultural heritage by thieves who have no comparable culture of their own! The demand has reached such proportions that it has now become a great international crime." His voice was angry. "I know of two areas of ruins in the northern jungles of Thailand that have been stripped bare. The ruins date back to one of our earliest kingdoms and were marked down for serious archaeological research. When our research team arrived they found that the ruins had been demolished, and the earth ripped open. Anything that had not been brutally looted had been carelessly destroyed!"

"Have you had any success in finding the people responsible?" I enquired gently.

"No!" the curt answer vibrated with more anger. Then it was controlled and he explained at more length. "These people must have local help, but to the poor villager in the hills the price of a rice sack can often mean more than the national heritage he does not yet understand. This makes the despoilers more difficult to catch."

"Regrettable, but understandable," I murmured softly.

The Inspector nodded. "But now I have a new approach, Mister Chan. The nature of your enquiries tells me that you believe yourself to be on the trail of the same, or a similar organization. And from the ferocity of the attack made upon your person, I am inclined to believe that you may be right."

He became silent, and watched me closely.

"Inspector Karachorn," I said at last. "You have been frank with me, and so I will try to be frank with you. Your suspicions and mine are in harmony, and I would like to help you. Unfortunately my suspicions, like yours, lack confirmation. So far my activities in Bangkok have been confined to visiting *Siam Antiquities* to talk with Mister Srivaji, who was a business partner of Mark Sanders, the man who was murdered in Hong Kong."

"I know nothing against Mister Srivaji," Karachorn said thoughtfully. "He is well known in Bangkok and his business is long established. There has never been any previous suggestion that he could be involved in any illicit dealing, but of course I shall now be making my own enquiries."

"What about the American, Jack Holden?" I asked casually. "That's the man who was with Belinda and Tracey on the river today." I smiled as I added, "It may be pure coincidence that he is involved at all. Belinda and Tracey usually manage to attract a large number of men who have only flirtation in mind."

Karachorn frowned. "I know nothing about this American, but rest assured that I shall find out."

We talked for another hour, but neither of us could offer any more towards the other's enlightenment. Finally there was nothing more to say, and after exchanging mutual promises to keep in touch, Karachorn took his leave. We parted with a firm but guarded handshake.

After the Thai Inspector had gone I sat thoughtfully back in my chair, and tried to reach an assessment of his character. His English was perfect. He was intelligent, cultured and strongly patriotic, and his bitterness towards the temple robbers who were ruthlessly despoiling his country's past was only partially concealed.

However, his visit left two points unexplained. He had brought no sergeant with him to make notes of our conversation, which seemed out of character for an officer so efficient, and seemed to suggest that possibly his visit had not been entirely official. The second point on which I had cause to ponder was that he seemed to have no previous knowledge of Jack Holden, and was clearly under the impression that *Siam Antiquities* had only one owner. That could merely mean that Holden had been lying to impress a couple of luscious girls, or alternatively his position as Srivaji's business partner had been kept very much in the background.

Gillian finally interrupted my reverie by knocking loudly on my door and telling me that I was already half an hour late for dinner. I accompanied her down to the hotel dining room and there joined Belinda and Tracey over a bottle of imported wine and an excellent meal of Thai cuisine. While we dined I told them about Karachorn's visit, and later we adjourned to the bar for an idle evening of discussion.

I had hopes that Jack Holden might appear, but in that respect the evening was wasted.

* * *

It seemed pointless to make a third visit to *Siam Antiquities*, and so the following morning I explored the only avenue of enquiry that was now left open. I gave Belinda and Tracey leave to indulge in a shopping spree, while I paid a call on one of the largest of Bangkok's magnificent array of temples. Gillian insisted on keeping me company.

The sun was high in a vivid blue sky when we entered the precincts of the gorgeous, glittering Wat Po Monastery. Here the temple courtyards were a maze of dazzling spires, broken up by occasional trees, palm fronds, walls and gateways, rock gardens and still, calm pools. Fearsome demons and grim bronze lions guarded every entrance, and there were innumerable shrines and grey stone *stupas* thrusting tapering needle points to the sky. The slanted, many-tiered roofs of the main buildings were brilliantly coloured with red and blue or green and orange tiles, while golden nagus, the celestial serpents, raised their horned heads from every apex. Altogether it made a superb composite picture of the rich variety of Thai art and architectural design.

Young Buddhist monks in the simple but highly predominant orange robes moved quietly among the flocks of visitors, and in the gloom of a vast pavilion beside the colossal gold-leafed figure of the reclining Buddha, I found a monk who spoke a little English. He held a scriptural text close to his chest with both hands as he listened carefully to my request, and then he nodded his shaven head in understanding and signed to us to follow his lead.

We returned to the blinding sunlight, and crossed a series of paved courtyards that led us away from the main buildings. Finally we reached a smaller and less elaborate building that provided simple residential quarters for the monks. An older man, very wizened in his orange robe, sat in silent contemplation with another book in his folded hands in the shade of the long verandah. Our guide begged us to wait, and then approached his senior with respect. After a brief exchange of words the older man looked towards us and nodded. The young monk signed to us to approach, smiled to us politely, and then discreetly moved away.

I sat down on the grass, facing the low verandah, and Gillian followed my example and sat by my side. The old monk put aside his book and picked up his spectacles from the lap of his orange robe. He donned the spectacles carefully, and then placed his palms together as he spoke in a soft voice.

"You are welcome here. The novice tells me that you wish to speak with a senior Bhikkhu who speaks English. The Abbot of this monastery is not here at this moment, but if I may offer my own humble assistance then I am at your service."

"Thank you," I answered quietly. "It is most kind of you to spare us time from your meditations."

"But how can I help?" he asked

sincerely. "Do you require spiritual advice?"

"Not exactly," I said, and I signed to Gillian to open her shoulder bag which she had placed on the lawn at her side. "My quest is a less noble one for information. I have a relic which I believe is of great devotional value, and I wish to return it to the altar of the temple to which it belongs. I hope that perhaps you can help me to find the rightful owners."

I showed him the green jade Buddha.

11

THE old Bikkhu gazed at the image calmly, with no sign of any great inner emotion or excitement. The humbled feelings that had been inspired in Belinda and myself, and even in the shrewd, materialistic soul of Srivaji, showed no reflection in the serene facc of the old man in the orange robe. A full minute passed before he held out his wrinkled brown hands, and the movement was gentle, with no haste, and not the faintest trembling of impatience or desire.

"Please," he said softly, "May I see the Buddha?"

I placed the image in his hands, and there was a long silence while he inspected it carefully with his weak eyes blinking slowly behind his plain spectacles. The sun was hot on our shoulders, and there was a distant murmur of hushed voices from the courtyards of the main temples. I felt relaxed and was content to wait for the old man's answer. It was very peaceful here.

"It is truly a wonderful Buddha," he said at last. "It is very old, and as you believe it is of a great devotional value. I can feel the many prayers that this Buddha has heard over the centuries. The surface is warm, where it has felt the touch of many Seekers of Enlightenment." He raised his shaven head of short grey stubble and regarded me gravely. "May I ask how you came by this image?"

"It is a very long story," I said quietly, "And perhaps most of it is unimportant. I do not know the source of its origin, but I fear that it must have been taken by force from a temple somewhere in Thailand. I seek only to return it."

For another full minute he stared gently into my eyes, as though he possessed the capability to read what was written in my soul. Then he nodded very slowly and returned the green jade Buddha to my hands.

"Only once have I ever seen a Buddha such as this one, carved in this style, and from this quality of jade stone, and with such ancient skill. That image was enshrined in the golden monastery of *Doy Suthep* that crowns the great hill that overlooks Chieng Mai. It is many years since I have travelled to Chieng Mai, and I have not heard that the image is missing from its shrine." He concluded apologetically. "I can tell you no more. In this quest, I do not know how I should advise you."

"Perhaps you have told me enough," I replied humbly. "I thank you for what you have said."

He smiled and nodded, and then closed his wise old eyes. I understood that the audience was over, and after a minute I rose silently to my feet. Gillian stood up beside me, she looked slightly baffled and so I took her hand and led her quietly away. When we reached the grey stone gateway that led to the main complex of temple buildings I paused to look back across the green lawn. The old Bikkhu in his orange robe sat cross-legged on his verandah as though he was already asleep. I knew that he had returned to his meditations, and the search for his own Enlightenment. Only if we had been engaged in a similar search could he have helped us more, for all lesser quests he could only regard as of no real concern. I regretted that I had been obliged to disturb his peace, and for a brief moment I viewed him with envy.

★ ★ ★

When we returned to the hotel we found Jack Holden sitting at the bar with Belinda and Tracey. The American wore another open-necked shirt, this time with a yellow and brown check pattern, and he swivelled easily on his bar stool when he heard our approach. His mouth stretched into a handsome grin, and again I felt a muted annoyance at his presence. I had expected and even hoped to see him again, but not to see him looking so complacently relaxed and familiar with my partners. I felt that my combined English and Chinese senses of refinement and courtesy were in some way affronted, and that like all insensitive Americans Jack Holden was just too sure of his own welcome.

"Hi, David. Hi, Gillian," he said cheerfully. "Come over and join us. Tracey was just saying that you ought to be back at any moment. What will you have to drink?"

It was too early for whisky so I accepted a cold beer. Gillian voted for a gin and tonic, having already acquired her first bad habit from Belinda and Tracey. Holden ensured that everyone had a full glass, and insisted that Gillian take over his bar stool which he promptly vacated. Gillian made an initial protest, then allowed herself to be placed uncertainly between Belinda and Tracey, like a shy rosebud between two fully developed blooms that were a joy and glory to the eye.

"Tracey has just been telling me what you're all doing here in Bangkok," Holden said at last when we were all settled. "I didn't know you were all private detectives, David." He became less voluble and lowered his glass to look more soberly at Gillian. "I also didn't know that Mark Sanders was your father. He was a good friend of mine, we had some good nights out together here in Bangkok. I couldn't believe it when I heard that he was dead — murdered — that just doesn't seem possible. Mark was such a decent guy, one of the best." He paused. "Gillian, I don't know how to begin to tell you how sorry I am."

Gillian nodded dumbly, and then looked down at her glass and bit her lip. Holden had sounded sincere and had reminded her of her grief, and she wasn't yet sure how to handle this situation. Because she couldn't answer I intervened and said casually,

"I suppose Tracey told you all about the murder?"

"Not all of it, she's just been filling in some of the details." Holden looked relieved, as if he too felt that my interruption had extricated him from an awkward moment, and he went on to explain: "Srivaji told me about Mark Sanders last night. It was a complete shock to me. You see, David, I've been away from Bangkok on a business trip for the past few days, so I didn't know anything about your visits. I only got back a couple of nights ago, and yesterday morning was the first time that I'd looked in at *Siam Antiquities* for over a week. I was intending to see Srivaji then, but I spotted Belinda and Tracey first, and I guess I allowed myself to get side-tracked." He grinned jointly at the two girls. "You certainly know how to surround yourself with beautiful women, David."

"They're not just pretty faces," I warned him. "They have smart brains too. All that I really contribute to the success of this agency is the occasional fit of violent leg-work and the office rent."

Belinda and Tracey exchanged dubious glances, but decided not to comment. For the moment they were too tactful to interrupt.

Holden chuckled briefly and then resumed his story.

"When that guy opened fire with his rifle I was amazed. At that time I just didn't know anything about what was happening. Your girls were discreet, David. They were getting more out of me than I was getting out of them. In terms of information I mean. I had just figured them as two really nice girls that I would like to know better. Anyway, when I did finally see Srivaji last night, I told him about the incident on the river. As soon as I mentioned the name of David Chan he burst in to tell me who you were, and why you were here in Bangkok. He also told me how Mark Sanders had been murdered in Hong Kong." He paused there and then finished, "I guess the girls have already told you enough to figure out that Mark, Srivaji and I were all known to each other through business relationships."

"I did gather that you were a business partner of Srivaji's," I conceded blandly.

Holden nodded. "That's right. I have some money invested in *Siam Antiquities*. I had no connection with *Exotic Art* in Hong Kong, that was a private deal between Srivaji and Mark Sanders. However, I knew Mark well enough. When he visited Bangkok I usually helped Srivaji to entertain him. Mark's trips always ended in a farewell dinner at one of the big hotels, a meal, plenty of wine, maybe some Thai dancing — " He paused to glance hesitantly at Gillian, and then added the rest. " — and usually a few invited girls."

Gillian failed to look shocked and Holden seemed relieved. However, he was leading me away from the point I wanted to clarify.

"Srivaji never mentioned anything about your part ownership in *Siam Antiquities*," I mused thoughtfully. "I wonder why?"

"I've no idea. There's no reason why it should be kept a secret. Srivaji's out of his depth in all this, so maybe he saw no relevance in it. I'm not sure that I can either." He smiled, but the smile looked hurt. "David, surely you don't rate me as a possible suspect in this case."

"No, Jack," I laughed as though the idea was ridiculous. "I'm just confused, that's all. We were surprised to find that Mark Sanders had one partner. Now we find that suddenly its a three-way partnership."

"Not exactly. Srivaji helped to set Mark Sanders up in Hong Kong years before I came on the scene. I had nothing to do with their deal and no place in it. I came out this way only a few years back, and spent two years with the U.S. Air Force flying Thunderchiefs out of Northern Thailand to hit the Ho Chi Minh trail in North Vietnam and Laos. Anyway, I reached the end of my time in the service, and I decided I wanted to stay on in Thailand. I liked the country, I liked the people, I even married a Thai girl."

He looked to Tracey as though he owed her a personal explanation about that. "We were only married for a year, then she got killed in a road accident."

"I'm sorry," Tracey said quietly.

Holden nodded and was silent for a moment. Then he took a long swallow from his beer and looked back to me.

"Anyway, David — about Srivaji. I'd quit the Air Force, I had a Thai wife, and I wanted to stay in a country I liked. I had some money to invest and I met Srivaji. At that time business was booming, there were thousands of

Americans visiting Bangkok regularly on R and R, and Srivaji wanted to expand quickly while the boom lasted. In the end I invested everything I had in *Siam Antiquities*." He leaned back and finished his beer. "That's all, David. I swear that's all there is to tell."

It seemed an appropriate moment to recharge the circle of now empty glasses, so I nodded agreeably and then suggested another round of drinks. While I ordered at the bar Holden turned his attention again to Gillian. He said a few comforting things about her father, expressing his sympathy once more, and offering any help that he could possibly give.

Gillian tugged at her lower lip with her teeth, her eyes downcast, but finally looked up to say in a low voice.

"All that I want, Mister Holden, is to find the man who murdered my father."

Holden frowned, and looked vaguely at Tracey. The silence continued until

I passed round the filled glasses, and then Holden said,

"I'll help in any way I can, if someone can show me a way." His grey eyes fixed on mine. "David, you've started this investigation — how do you intend to go on from here?"

I hesitated, as though I needed time to weigh up my decision, and then I reached for Gillian's shoulder bag and showed him the green jade Buddha.

"This is the only positive line of enquiry that we have," I told him quietly. "A man who ran away from Sander's villa in Hong Kong was trying to steal it. Belinda and I believe that it must have been stolen originally in Thailand, and so this morning I showed it to a senior monk at the Wat Po monastery. He remembers a similar image being on display at Chieng Mai, and so Chieng Mai is my next destination. If I can find out where this Buddha came from, then I can possibly determine how it came to be in Sander's possession, and from there start closing in on the man who committed murder in his efforts to retrieve it."

Holden stared at the jade figure, and I sensed that he knew its value. He made no move to touch the image, but at the same time there was a tension in him which suggested that he was making a physical effort to resist the temptation. I watched him, and had to remind myself that as another dealer in antiquities he would naturally be able to recognize a piece that was priceless. His knowledge was no cause for suspicion.

"Are you sure this can lead you to the murderer?" He finally asked.

"I'm sure that it points to a trail that I must follow."

"Then I think that I'd best accompany you up north to Chieng Mai." He looked up and continued quickly to stall any possible protests. "I've just promised Gillian that I'll do anything to help — and I owe it to her father. Mark Sanders was a good friend of mine."

"It's not really necessary," I said mildly.

"But I still want to come along. I know Chieng Mai well, and that local knowledge could be useful. Also I speak Thai like a native, and that's another asset you might not find amiss."

That surprised me. "On the river yesterday you showed no sign of speaking the language!"

Holden laughed. "You bet your sweet life I didn't. There are times when it's better not to know the language, and yesterday was one of them. I couldn't have told those police guys anything anyway." He dismissed the topic and demanded bluntly, "How do you propose to travel north?"

"By train."

"Thai Airways flies daily. Chieng Mai is the northern capital."

"I know, but I intend to take the girls along, and as Gillian is paying all our expenses I don't want to hit her with any excessive air fares. The express train will be comfortable enough."

"Alright," Holden decided not to argue. "We'll take the express train. And I'm definitely coming with you, David. After that incident on the river I reckon you may well need some extra male help to look after these three gorgeous girls!"

He smiled as he spoke, but the smile was directed specifically at Tracey, and I knew that his taste in women was for flame red hair and emerald green eyes.

"We'll be glad to have you, Jack." Tracey returned his smile.

That was enough for Jack Holden, and as far as he was concerned he was an accepted member of our party. He drained his beer and stood up briskly, the committed man of action.

"I'll check the train departures and the fares," he said. "It won't take a minute."

He left the bar and went out to the hotel reception desk. There he spoke briefly with the little Thai girl on duty, and I saw her smile pleasantly at him as she picked up the white telephone and began to dial a number on his behalf. I watched him for a moment, and then looked back to the three girls. They were all regarding me with various degrees of enquiry in their eyes.

"David," Gillian broke the silence softly. "Do you think he is on our side? After all, you've told him everything we intend to do."

"Give a man enough rope," I said solemnly, "And if he is dishonest he will weave a noose to fit his own neck."

"David thinks that is another ancient Chinese proverb," Belinda told Gillian disparagingly. "But as you and I well know it's a distortion from the English."

"Then that must be one of the few I learned from my mother," I said without blinking.

Only Tracey failed to smile at the exchange. "What makes you think that Jack might be dishonest?" she demanded curtly. "I'm sure that he could not have had any part in that attack on the river. Belinda and I had only met him a few minutes before, he didn't really know any of us, and I'll swear that he was unaware that anything was going to happen."

"That's true," I agreed. "But the man who was in the most likely position to have planned that attack on Gillian and myself has to be Srivaji. And Jack Holden is Srivaji's business associate and partner."

Tracey remained unconvinced, and suddenly I realized that the attraction she held for Holden was at least mutual and in some part returned. At the same time I admitted to myself that the concealed dislike I maintained for the American had nothing to do with my affronted inner sensitivity, of either Chinese or English heritage. Instead it was just plain, old-fashioned sexual jealousy.

12

AT noon the following day we boarded the north-bound express for Chieng Mai at Bangkok's sprawling central railway station. Jack Holden accompanied us, true to his word, and dispensing generous tips to taxi drivers and porters all round. The platforms were a surging tangle of humanity, familiar to railway stations the world over at busy departure moments, but we eventually sorted ourselves out into a first class, air-conditioned compartment. Holden and I stowed an assortment of small travelling suitcases into the luggage rack, and had barely settled ourselves when the train started to move. In the same moment we realized that we had company, for another passenger, moving along the corridor stared in at our party and then decided to join us.

He was a big, heavy man of about fifty, and obviously another American. He was running to fat and sweating inside a lightweight grey suit, and his face was ugly with a broken-toothed grin. It was a face that a woman might find repellent or attractive, depending on whether she considered good looks effeminate. He pushed his way inside and dropped heavily into a vacant seat beside Belinda.

"Hell, it's good to find some real American faces . . . " He spoke to Holden and grinned at the girls. "I hope you folks don't mind my company, because I'd sure rather travel with fellow-Americans than with a pack of natives."

Holden looked as though he did object, and glancing unobtrusively at his face I felt a moment of malicious satisfaction. Holden was quite happy to crowd in on my girls, but he had an equal resentment for any other intruder hoping to cut in on the same game. He offered no immediate welcome, but his lack of response went unnoticed.

"The name's Rickhardt," our new companion barged on brashly. "Gus Rickhardt. I'm from Detroit, Michigan!"

"Jack Holden. Denver, Colorado," Holden said reluctantly.

Rickhardt thrust out a large, hairy paw, and he and Holden shook hands. However, Rickhardt was already looking at the girls.

"Tracey Ryan," Tracey said, "From New York City."

She went on to introduce the rest of the party, and Rickhardt beamed his broken-toothed grin of acknowledgement at both Gillian and Belinda. In my direction he spared only the briefest nod.

"I'm with Chevrolet." Rickhardt patted the brown leather briefcase he had brought with him as though it were some kind of badge of office. "Chief Salesman for this part of the world. We're trying to break into a larger slice of the Asian market, but it's a hard grind. The God-damned

Japs are flooding the place with their lousy little Toyotas and all that crap." He spared me another glance. "Say, I hope you're not a Jap."

"I'm part Chinese," I told him softly.

"Oh, a Chink!"

"The word is Chinese."

My tone was even softer, but more final. I was crushing down the slow inner urge to dislodge a few more of his teeth with a gentle karate chop across the mouth, and some of the steel must have showed through in my eyes. Rickhardt decided not to push it and grunted a one word apology.

The train left the modern city of Bangkok, and as the last block of flats disappeared behind us the landscape became completely agricultural, row after row of long vegetable plots forming huge, wide-furrowed fields. The small signs of rural habitation that we passed were mostly shanty towns of wooden walls roofed with rusting brown tin, and usually they straddled a small river or canal. Only Rickhardt found it uninteresting, and he tried to engage Belinda in conversation. Belinda smiled at him coolly but gave him no real encouragement, and finally he tired of the effort. He pulled a pint hip flask from his pocket and offered it around the compartment.

"Anyone care for a drink, it's real American bourbon." He grinned. "I wouldn't drink the local Thai stuff. They call it Mekong, and that's exactly what it tastes like — a drop of lousy Mekong river water!"

Holden accepted a brief drink from the flask, probably because he felt it would be rude to refuse a fellow-American. The rest of us declined, and on the second offer Holden made the excuse the he never did any serious drinking in the mid-afternoon heat. Rickhardt shrugged and seemed unoffended. He drank alone, and gradually renewed his unsuccessful efforts to strike up a friendly relationship with Belinda.

★ ★ ★

Throughout the afternoon the train roared north, passing between yellowed fields of harvested rice stubble, and marshy green pools that floated lotus leaves and aquatic bird life. Buffaloes and cows, once an old woman shooing geese, and a few peasants in their wide straw hats were the only signs of movement between the towns. This was the dry season, and the flat land that would later be wet and green with young rice shoots, now had a barren, sun-baked look.

At every stop the train was besieged by smiling food and drink vendors who ran busily up and down the platforms. They sold everything from dried fish on sticks to hot meals on leaf plates, plus oranges, pineapple chunks, peanuts, and bamboo tubes stuffed with sweetened coconut rice. To wash it all down they offered palm juice and iced coffee in small plastic bags. Holden and Rickhardt began to compete with each other in buying select tit-bits for the girls, and the journey began to develop into one long party. Gillian revealed an insatiable appetite for every new delicacy that was discovered, and Holden and Tracey became more content with each other's company.

Gus Rickhardt drank his way through his pint of bourbon without showing any ill effects. He merely sweated more profusely and talked more loudly. His conversation was mostly about Gus Rickhardt, and Detroit, and the problems of selling real size automobiles for the lousy back roads of Asia. After his first calculating survey of the girls he seemed to acknowledge that Tracey and Holden were together, and so his talk was mostly directed at Gillian and Belinda. It was Gillian who showed the biggest response, but it was Belinda whom he wanted to impress. I closed my eyes and pretended to doze, listening carefully to all that was said throughout the afternoon and early evening, but none of it was important.

By seven o'clock darkness had descended behind a swift blaze of sunset. A white-coated waiter from the dining car served us with hot meals of rice, egg and meat, followed by coffee. At the same time Rickhardt persuaded the waiter to refill his hip flask with another pint of bourbon. After the meal he began to drink again, and this time it was difficult not to join him. Holden finally capitulated, perhaps reasoning that it was best not to let Rickhardt drink another full pint.

When the hip flask was empty for the second time Tracey and Belinda exchanged private glances. It was now getting late and Belinda nodded. Tracey yawned lazily, and Belinda remarked that Gillian looked tired. Gillian looked startled, for she was in fact still bright-eyed and lively, and Rickhardt made a sluggish protest. However, Tracey and Belinda had decided, and the party broke up.

We adjourned to separate sleeping compartments for the rest of the night journey, and although Rickhardt endeavoured to detain Belinda for a while longer, my English Rose had the mechanics of the polite freeze polished to a fine art. She bid him goodnight with her sweetest smile, and left him before he could decide upon the best approach.

While the express roared on through the night into the invisible hills of Northern Thailand, I lay wide awake in my sleeper bunk and pondered on the possible significance of Gus Rickhardt's imposed presence in our midst. My thinking brought forth no answers, and finally the rocking motion of the train lulled me into a comfortable sleep.

★ ★ ★

At dawn the next morning we arrived at Chieng Mai, five hundred miles north of Bangkok. The girls were wide awake when Holden and I emerged from our sleeping compartment, but of Gus Rickhardt there was no sign. I guessed that he was probably suffering from a hangover, and as we had no call to wait for him Holden and I got our suitcases organized on to the platform. Once through the ticket barrier there were eager taxi drivers to relieve us of our burdens. Holden and Tracey took one taxi, and I took Belinda and Gillian in another. We drove to the New Oriental Hotel, where Holden had telephoned ahead to book rooms in advance.

Chieng Mai was an attractive little city, built in the shadow of green Mount Suthep, and overlooked by the golden gleam of the high monastery I had come to visit. The older part of the city, once a royal capital, was built in a large square inside dark green canals that had once formed a great moat, a double protection to complement the the original city walls which had long since collapsed. Inside the old city were time-mellowed temples, less splendid and eye-searing than those of Bangkok, but infinitely more restful. The New Oriental Hotel was on the bank of the Mae Ping River, which wended a shallow course through the more modern part of the city.

We started the day with a large breakfast, and then spent the rest of the morning unpacking and installing ourselves in the rooms provided. The girls all insisted that they needed long hot baths after the fifteen hour journey, and so it was obvious that nothing could be accomplished until after noon.

At five past twelve I descended to the hotel bar, and found that Belinda at least had put in an appearance. She looked fresh and sparkling in a wine-red blouse and a slim black skirt. She sat with her legs crossed casually on a leather-topped bar stool, but she was not alone. Gus Rickhardt had followed us from the train and was now parked on the seat beside her.

A bar tender served them with two iced drinks, the inevitable bourbon for Rickhardt and a gin and tonic for Belinda. While Rickhardt turned to the bar to sign the bill, Belinda acknowledged me with a smile.

"Hi, David."

"Hi," I said. And then to Rickhardt, "Good morning, Gus."

Rickhardt nodded briefly, but then turned his shoulder to exclude me from their conversation.

"How about it, Belinda," he pressed her. "Just you and me. I know Chieng Mai like the back of my own hand. I've been here a hundred times. I can show you everything you want to see. Temples — there's lots of temples here. And a waterfall, on that big green hill out there they have a waterfall."

"I'll think about it," Belinda said calmly. "It's too early for sight-seeing. I've barely got off the train."

I attracted the bar tender's attention. It was obvious that nobody was going to offer me a drink, so I ordered my own beer. Behind me Rickhardt continued to argue.

"Okay, tomorrow then. I can pick you up tomorrow."

Belinda was smiling sadly, and made a negative move of her dark head.

"Aw, come on, Doll — don't give Old Gus the brush-off. I'm not used to that cold shoulder stuff!"

He waited for a more favourable response, but none came. The bar tender placed my beer in front of me, almost silently, but the movement caused Rickhardt to twist round on his seat and glare into my face. He was uglier than ever, and this morning he was belligerent.

"Hey, you're listening in on a private conversation," he snarled sourly. "Why don't you move further off along the bar?"

I paused with one hand on my beer and said calmly, "One section of a bar is much like any other. This section will suit me."

Rickhardt climbed down from his stool and planted his hairy-backed hands on his fat hips.

"Don't get smart with me, you wise-ass little Chink!"

I replaced my beer gently on the counter and turned to face him. He was so obvious he was ridiculous, and even though I knew he intended to get me mad I could feel my anger rising to the bait.

"Chinese," I reminded him. "The word is Chinese."

"Chink!" Rickhardt said, and he turned his broken-toothed grin towards Belinda. Whether he expected approval or protest it was difficult to tell, but he was plainly baffled by her complete lack of concern. The grin faltered and he glared back at me.

Belinda sighed wisely. "Don't hurt him, David," she said as though she didn't really care.

It was Rickhardt who got mad. "Chink!" he shouted and pushed hard at my shoulder.

I drove a fist smartly into his stomach, which was what he intended. I knew that I wasn't the first that he had goaded into throwing the opening punch, and he had enough fat there to cushion the blow. I didn't do him any damage, and it was all the excuse he wanted to draw back his shoulder and let fly with a massive bunch of knuckles that would have smashed my smile beyond repair. That was what I intended, and as I swayed to avoid the blow I turned under his arm, pulled down on his wrist, and hurled his fat, clumsy body clear across the room.

He hit the opposite wall with a crash that rattled every glass and bottle in the place. For a moment he sat there with the wind squeezed out of him and a blank look on his ugly face, then he struggled up, cursing horribly. He paused on one knee, dug a hand into his coat pocket, and pulled out a heavy brass knuckleduster that he started to slip over his right fist.

"You stinking little sonofabitch," he grated. "In Vietnam I killed hundreds of slit-eyed little runts like you."

I stepped forward and demonstrated

a neat boxing kick. The toe of my shoe hooked the brass knuckles out of his hands before he could slip them over his fingers. Bewilderment registered on his face, and then fury. I stepped back to give him plenty of room to charge.

He didn't disappoint me. He heaved his bulk to his feet and rushed me full tilt with all the bellowing force of a buffalo with a queen bee under its tail. I turned on the ball of my left foot, lashed back with my right heel and took him square in the crotch. He screamed in agony as he stumbled past, and I completed my pivoting motion in a full circle and let the momentum add extra speed to the hand chop that thudded into the back of his thick neck. Rickhardt went down like a felled tree, and this time he stayed down.

I rubbed the edge of my palm gently, and for a moment I feared that I had miscalculated the thickness of that bull neck and killed him. Then Belinda moved over to inspect the sprawled heap and affirmed that he was still alive.

"You didn't quite break his neck," she assured me. She frowned and added, "He's been trying hard to provoke you ever since we met. I wonder why he was so determined to start that fight."

"Perhaps he thought he could win," I suggested blandly. "After all, if I hadn't ducked his first punch I wouldn't now be in any position to carry on our investigation. It's not easy to ask nosey questions with a broken jaw."

13

THE noise of the disturbance brought Gillian running into the bar room. She stopped abruptly full of alarm with her blue eyes wide and wondering. Then Holden and Tracey appeared behind her. Holden looked almost as startled, and only Tracey arrived without haste and without surprise. She gave me a sad look of knowing reproach.

"What happened to Gus?" Holden demanded.

"I think he was trying to immobilize me," I apologized.

"Why the hell would he want to do that?"

"Maybe he really does hate Chinks."

Holden stared down at his fellow-American, and then shrugged his shoulders and gave a helpless shake of his head. "I guess he must be more sour with a hangover than he is when he's drinking."

The fracas had also attracted the attention of the entire hotel staff, and for a few moments we were surrounded by polished round faces that had temporarily lost their polite calm. The agitation was led by the hotel manager, and in the excitement even he had forgotten his English. Holden rapidly soothed them in their own language, and then turned back to me.

"This guy is full of apologies, although I don't know quite how he figures that it's his fault. Anyway, he says that Rickhardt does have a room booked here, so they want to get him up to it out of the way."

The bar tender and two waiters were already trying to lift Rickhardt's unconscious bulk, like three Lilliputians struggling with a gross Gulliver. Holden felt obliged to help.

"I'll give them a hand," he said.

I watched as Rickhardt was carried away. The manager fluttered beside me for a few more anxious moments, but when I assured him that I was unharmed and had no complaint against the hotel he finally followed the cortege. The incident was over and the remaining waiters and the girls from the reception desk drifted away. Tracey regarded me with an expression of mock severity, borrowed from Belinda for the occasion.

"David, I suppose that was unavoidable?"

I nodded solemnly.

Tracey remained thoughtful. "I suppose there's no point in contacting Chevrolet Motors to ask if they do have a Chief Salesman named Gus Rickhardt?"

"A complete waste of time," I assured her. "A salesman cultivates a friendly approach as a matter of habit, because he always hopes to sell something. Rickhardt hasn't got the right temperament for the job."

"Then what is he doing out here in Thailand?"

"When he wakes up, perhaps we'll get the opportunity to ask him."

The dialogue terminated with Holden's return. He came down the stairs with an uncomfortable look fitted on to his face, as though he felt in some way responsible for Rickhardt's behaviour.

"He's still out cold," he said. "And it's my guess he'll stay that way for at least an hour. I persuaded the manager not to make a big fuss by calling the police. I figured you wouldn't want that, David."

"It would be a nuisance," I admitted. "I want to get out to that monastery this afternoon, and I won't do it if I'm held up talking to the police."

Holden nodded, and put a casual arm around Tracey's waist.

"What about the rest of us, David? Is there anything we can do?"

"There could be. I've been meaning to ask you whether Mark Sanders was ever in the habit of visiting Chieng Mai?"

"Sometimes." Holden shrugged as

though he had never considered that it might be important. "A lot of Thai handicrafts are produced here in Chieng Mai. That's why I make frequent trips up here, Srivaji doesn't like to leave Bangkok, so I usually tour the factories and place the orders for *Siam Antiquities*. A lot of Mark's stock came from here, through Srivaji, and so he had an interest in seeing how it was made. Also it's a lot less humid here than it is in Bangkok. Mark's been up here a few times. A couple of times he's made the trip with me."

"That's a help," I acknowledged. "Maybe you and Tracey could cover some of that old ground, talk to the people who might remember Mark Sanders, anyone he might have done business with. You know the places to go, and Tracey knows the right questions to ask. Together you might come up with something. In the meantime I'll take Gillian and Belinda with me to the monastery."

The opportunity to work with Tracey

suited Holden fine, and he made no objections. We talked for another half hour, and then the hotel manager suddenly appeared showing more agitation. Holden listened to him for a moment, and a flicker of annoyance crossed his face.

"Damnit," Holden exploded. "This guy tells me that Gus Rickhardt has cleared out of the hotel. He must have woken up a lot sooner than I expected. He packed his bag, gave the room boy ten dollars to cover his bill, and left ten minutes ago!"

It seemed that Rickhardt had neatly vanished. He hadn't made the mistake of hailing a taxi within sight of the New Oriental, so there was no way of discovering his next destination. I dismissed the subject for an hour while we enjoyed a meal, and then persuaded the girl receptionist to make a series of enquiring telephone calls. We learned that Rickhardt had not booked into any other hotel, and neither had he showed his face at the railway station or the airport. I deduced that he had gone to ground somewhere in Chieng Mai, but until he decided to re-emerge I could only comment with regret on his prompt powers of recuperation, and accept his escape with philosophical calm.

★ ★ ★

There was no point in delaying our original plans, so during the afternoon I hired a taxi to take Belinda, Gillian and myself up the steep winding road that climbed Mount Suthep to the golden temple and monastery that overlooked Chieng Mai from a height of three-thousand, five-hundred feet. It was a beautiful excursion, the road ascending through green jungle depths, twice passing small waterfalls that tumbled down the mountainside. Bright red flowers and orange-blossomed creepers abounded in the sun-pierced woods.

Belinda had been absorbing the local history from the informative hotel manager, and was able to tell us that the road had been hewn out of the jungle slopes by an army of five thousand volunteers led by a divinely-inspired monk. Before that the temple had been accessible only to those devotees who were physically fit.

When the road ended a flight of steep steps began, flanked on either side by dark green pine trees. We left the taxi behind and began the climb, and after two turns through the pines we found two magnificent *nagas*, the seven-headed serpents of Thai mythology, rearing up to protect the final flight of three hundred steps. The naga guardians were twice as tall as ourselves, and their undulating green and gold snake bodies continued right up to the golden temple on the summit of the hill.

There were in fact two red and gold temples, their steep, three-tiered tiled roofs crowned with horned *nagas*, at every corner and apex. Between the two temples rose a great golden *stupa*, rising to a lofty spire piercing the blue heaven. In the cloisters encircling the temple compound were rows of life size Buddha images, all silent and serene in the shadowed gloom. Beyond the holy place was a superb aerial view of Chieng Mai, spread out like a flat map in a vast heat haze that obscured the far horizons.

I followed the procedure I had employed at the Wat Po in Bangkok, and again sought out a senior monk. With his grey, shaven head, his wrinkled hands, and his identity lost in the bright anonymity of his orange robe, he could almost have been a twin brother of the old Bhikkhu who had started me on my quest. His composure was identical, and when I showed him the green jade Buddha he examined it in the same calm, unhurried manner.

"I have been told that this image may belong here at Doy Suthep," I explained quietly. "If this is it's rightful place, then I wish to return it to the temple."

The old monk was silent for a long moment, and then at last he looked up at my face and rejected the Buddha. Uncertainly I accepted its return.

"Please follow me," he said, and turned away.

We followed him into the large temple that faced the golden *stupa*. Inside a massive gilded Buddha held the place of honour before the altar where flower vases were arranged and sticks of incense gave off sweet smoke. The huge standing Buddha dominated the shrine, but before it on the highest part of the altar was a small Buddha in the cross-legged position of meditation. The smaller Buddha was only six inches high, and carved from green jade. It was identical to the figure I held in my hands.

"Here is our Buddha." The old monk spoke carefully because his grasp of English was slight. "As you see, it has not been stolen."

Belinda and Gillian looked perplexed, and I felt disappointment that the trail had finished in a dead end. I was about to thank him when he turned slowly and continued:

"There is a small village, twenty miles north east of this place. It is called Chandi. I know that in Chandi temple there was a Buddha such as this — and that Buddha has been taken from its place. I think you must go to Chandi."

★ ★ ★

The old monk sent for a young novice with some knowledge of English to accompany us. Our guide was a slender youth named Chula who volunteered at once, and so with our new companion the girls and I returned to our taxi. The seating arrangements needed a little tact, because the monk was not permitted to sit touching a woman. Finally I squashed into the back of the taxi between Gillian and Belinda, and with Chula seated happily beside the driver we were able to depart.

We descended the mountain, and then headed north on the twenty mile journey that took us into the jungle-covered foothills that approached the rugged mountain ranges of the Burma border. For the last few miles we left the main road to bump over a dirt track through tangled forest. Chula assured us that here tiger, leopard bear and wild boar still roamed freely. It was a land of dark ranges, peopled sparsely by a few wandering hill tribes and hunters.

We came at last to Chandi, a small huddle of poor huts that barely qualified for the title of a village. However, it boasted a small temple beside a weathered *stupa* of bare grey stone. The resident priest was the oldest monk I had yet seen, so frail that he looked like a yellowed parchment doll in his orange robe. He approached us on worn sandals as though the weight of his years was almost more than he could bear. His shrunken face showed only bewilderment at the sight of such a large party arriving unexpectedly on his doorstep.

Chula bowed low, giving the old man the veneration that was his due. He explained our presence, but still the old man failed to understand. I showed him the green jade Buddha, and then suddenly everything was clear. My search was over, for large tears began to trickle out of the failing eyes, and the old priest of Chandi wept without shame.

We waited until he had recovered his composure enough to thank us. His gratitude and Chula's smiles could not be hurried, and I answered their questions as much as I was able.

"Chula," I intervened at last. "Please ask him how the Buddha came to be stolen?"

Chula nodded and interpreted the question. The old priest listened and became silent at the memory. Emotion made his thin shoulders tremble, and finally he answered with a low monologue. When Chula translated the misty old eyes were fixed on mine.

"The Learned Bhikkhu says that the Buddha was taken many weeks ago. Bad men came to Chandi in the night and robbed the temple. With the jade Buddha they took the bronze incense holders, and the golden flower bowls from the altar. They stripped everything that could be moved. They were men of great evil and no compassion."

The old Bhikkhu spoke again, his quavering voice addressed directly to me. When he stopped Chula repeated his words with a horrified sadness.

"The Learned Bhikkhu says that a monk was killed by these evil men. He was a boy novice like myself, and his name was Muang." He paused to explain. "In Thailand every young boy is expected to spend at least three months of his life in a monastery. Some young men stay much longer, and some remain for all their lives, but three months is the minimum. The boy Muang was in his first month, and he discovered the robbers as they violated the temple. The bad men murdered him to stop his cries before they fled." He shook his head and shared the old man's sorrow. "It was a black day for Chandi, when their temple was robbed bare, and the boy Muang was murdered."

"They were indeed terrible crimes," I agreed quietly. "Now I wish to find the men who committed these crimes and bring them to justice. Will you ask the Learned Bhikkhu if there is anything more that he can tell about the temple robbers? Were any of their faces seen?"

Chula relayed the question, and the old priest of Chandi looked disturbed. His weak eyes studied us all in turn, and then he looked down at the jade Buddha which was still held with reverence in his hands.

He had a difficult decision to make, but at last he began to speak.

"The Learned Bhikkhu says that there is a very old temple deep in the jungle," Chula translated and pointed an uncertain finger towards the western hills. "It is a ruin many hundreds of years old which the jungle has almost reclaimed. Only a few of the hunters who search afar for game know where it is to be found."

He had to make frequent stops to listen to the old man's faltering words, but slowly the story unfolded.

"There have been other ruins, also as ancient, which the Government wanted to examine, and then perhaps show them to the Western tourists. Those ruins were invaded and destroyed by the temple robbers before the Government people could make their inspection. So this last place has been kept a secret. This Learned Bhikkhu has told no one, because he fears that if the Government knows, so the bad men will find out and despoil the sacred places as before. Now, because you have returned the Chandi Buddha to its shrine, this Learned Bhikkhu is telling you all that he knows."

There was a longer pause, a more

detailed explanation, and finally we came to the point involved. Chula nodded and went on carefully:

"Also this Learned Bhikkhu fears that the place of these secret ruins has already been discovered. He has heard from the hill peoples that strangers have been seen and heard near the ancient remains."

"Were they white strangers, or Thai people?"

There was another exchange in Thai.

"One was a white stranger," Chula said at last. "The others were Thai, but not from these northern hills."

"Would there be any valuable relics, of gold or of jade, in these ruins of which the Learned Bhikkhu speaks?"

The question needed discussion, but finally Chula nodded.

"It is possible they are buried. The robbers dig up all the earth with spades. Also from the other ruins the robbers stole everything, the stone guardians, the carved doorways, even the walls and every shaped stone were removed."

"That fits the known pattern," Belinda advised me quietly. "It's happened to the Maya sites in Central America, and I've even heard rumours that the great temples of Angkor in Cambodia are being broken up piece by piece. The museum market takes everything, carved frieze panels, lintels, life-sized statues-anything that can be moved by a truck."

I asked a few more questions but there was nothing more to be learned. It was getting late, with the shadows lengthening between the distant ridges of jungle, and so we took our leave. The green jade Buddha I saw for the last time in the still unbelieving hands of the grateful old priest of Chandi, and we hurried to return Chula to Doy Suthep before nightfall.

14

IT was seven o'clock when we at last returned to Chieng Mai and the New Oriental Hotel, and Tracey and Jack Holden were still absent. I heard a second taxi pull up an hour later, and from my window I saw them leave the car and enter the foyer. I waited another ten minutes until I heard Holden singing and splashing cheerfully in the shower, and then I took a silent walk along the corridor to the room Tracey was sharing with Belinda. Gillian was already there, and all three were seated on the two single beds. Belinda had just finished speaking when I entered, and I guessed that she had been telling Tracey about our trip to Chandi.

"So you found the rightful owner of the jade Buddha," Tracey said, adding a smile to the compliment. "Now at least we know how and when it was stolen. All we have to learn now is how did it reach Hong Kong, and come into the hands of Mark Sanders?"

"I'm working on some theories," I promised her.

"My father paid for that Buddha!" Gillian fiercely re-affirmed her belief. "Even if it was stolen I'm sure he bought it in good faith!"

"It's still possible," I conceded.

Gillian glared at me bitterly, as though I had failed her.

"We're not really getting anywhere, are we?" she accused. "All these visits to temples, and finding out where the Buddha came from — it's all been a waste of time. We still don't know who killed my father!"

"Detection is a slow business," I soothed her gently. "You never find all the answers in the same place and at the same time. Collecting enough facts to build up a complete picture can take weeks, months, or even years. So far we've made a promising start."

Gillian still looked sulky, for patience was not one of her greatest virtues. However, I knew that her youthful spirit would soon bounce back, and so I turned to Tracey.

"How was your day with Jack Holden?"

"Very pleasant," Tracey smiled. "I enjoyed every minute of it. We spent the first hour or so looking around the art shops in Chieng Mai. Jack knew most of the shopkeepers he'd done business with many of them in the past for Siam Antiquities. Some of the dealers also remembered Mark Sanders from his last visit, and we found one man who recalled making him a direct sale of a set of hand-carved coffee tables that took his fancy. It all sounded routine and innocent enough."

"No one sold him the jade Buddha?"

Tracey shook her head. "No one admitted to the sale." She paused, and then continued her story: "After we had toured the art shops Jack suggested that we moved on to visit some of the local industries where the various handicrafts are made. He said that Mark Sanders had visited a few of these factories, so it seemed as good an occupation as any. All the little villages around here are devoted to their own particular trade. At one place we saw nothing but more silk factories, and at another it seemed that everybody in the village was making nothing but hand-painted paper sunshades. Then there was a silverware village, and a lacquerware village. We spent the whole afternoon driving around the countryside in a taxi. Watching all those craftsmen at work was quite fascinating."

"Did anyone in the village remember Mark Sanders?"

She shrugged. "It was much the same story that we heard in the art shops. A few of the factory owners recalled his visit, and in two cases he placed specific orders for their products to be sent via Srivaji."

I nodded slowly, because it was

pretty much what I had expected. "Did you visit any pottery factories?" I asked.

Tracey eyed me curiously, and then nodded in turn.

"There were about four grouped around one of the little villages. We inspected one of them and watched the different stages of manufacture. Once the clay image is moulded and carved they bake it in kilns. Then it gets handpainted and polished to a gloss finish . . . "

"Was Sanders known there?"

She shook her head.

"Even so, I'd like to see one of those factories for myself." I said thoughtfully. "Could you take me back to that pottery village?"

"Sure, tomorrow morning if you like."

"I was thinking in terms of a more clandestine visit," I explained blandly. "Tonight, while the premises are closed — and preferably now, before Jack Holden gets out of the shower."

Tracey viewed me with suspicion. "Jack and I were going out to dinner. We found a sweet little place where we can dine with subdued lights and soft music. Afterwards I'm sure he hopes to make love to me!"

"Belinda can stall Jack for you," I said hopefully.

Tracey smiled, and a hint of mischief sparkled in her emerald eyes. "Perhaps I don't want him stalled. I might welcome his advances."

I was silent, and my pained loss of words brought forth a mass burst of laughter in which even Gillian shared.

"David," Belinda observed, "Behind that English stiff upper lip, and that inscrutable Chinese smile, you really are human after all!"

"Human enough to be jealous," Tracey chuckled. "David, I am flattered."

I had no option but to wait while they enjoyed their joke, but finally Tracey made a concession.

"I don't know why you're interested

in a village that makes pottery, but just for old times' sake I'll let Belinda stall Jack while I show you the way."

★ ★ ★

We left immediately, because I wanted Holden to have no opportunity for asking awkward questions in advance. Also on this occasion I felt that we could do without the inconvenient presence of a taxi-driver, and so I hired a self-drive car from the hotel. The reception staff were too polite to show any of the curiosity they might have felt, and so there was no need for explanations. The car was provided promptly and we drove away.

I handled the wheel while Tracey navigated. Once clear of Chieng Mai the headlights showed dry yellow rice fields fading swiftly into darkness, but the distance was not far and Tracey had a good memory for the road. After less than twenty minutes a twinkle of lights glowed ahead, only slightly more brilliant than the stars that were half obscured by slow-passing clouds.

"That's it," Tracey said calmly. "That's the pottery village."

I turned the car off the road, bumping on to the grass verge and stopping in the black pool of shadow cast by a large tree. There I switched off the engine and the lights.

"The car will attract too much attention," I said regretfully. "We'll have to walk the last half mile."

"My expenses will include a new pair of shoes," Tracey warned me, but she made no real complaint.

We walked for another ten minutes along the darkened road before we came to the edge of the village. It was a small collection of neatly thatched wooden houses and shuttered souvenir shops. It had a much more prosperous air than Chandi, and the spacing of the buildings was well regulated with flowering shrubs and shade trees. A dog barked once, but visitors were frequent here and the rest of the canine population were too complacent to rouse themselves merely to sound an alarm for strangers. After the first fitful yelps the one exception decided that he too couldn't be bothered and fell silent.

"That's the factory we visited this afternoon."

Tracey pointed out a long, shed-like building that was dimly visible on our right. I made a negative motion of my head.

"That's not the one I want."

"There's another one beyond it, but that was receiving visitors too. I saw a couple of tour cars there."

"Then it won't be that one either."

"We drove through the village on our way out. There are two more pottery factories on the far side. I didn't see any sign that they were open to casual visitors. There were no tour cars, and no welcome notices."

"That sounds more promising," I allowed. "But I don't think we could walk through the main street without being noticed. We'll have to circle round."

"I must be mad," Tracey said. "Giving up a romantic dinner just to go hiking over rice fields in the middle of the night."

"It could be worse," I consoled her. "In the wet season we would be paddling instead of hiking, and think of how that rich food would have spoiled your hour-glass figure."

"I'm thinking," Tracey said gloomily. But she accompanied me anyway.

It took us another fifteen minutes to make a wide circle of the village, and then we stopped again in the shadow of an ancient mango tree on the far side. Here Tracey pointed out the two remaining factories. One was situated close to the road emerging from the village, the other was a little further away and surrounded by a solid stone wall six feet high.

"My instinct tells me to aim for the building that is best protected," I said quietly. "You can wait for me here."

"For how long, David?"

"Don't worry, I'll be back within an hour."

She looked doubtful, but she didn't argue. I left her beneath the mango tree and continued alone, moving faster but with more stealth. I used the cover that was available, more mango trees, a clump of tamarind, and for a few yards a narrow irrigation channel which concealed me at a crouch. There was no sound as I approached the wall.

I made sure that there were no wires, barbed or electric, running along the top of the wall, and then I heaved myself nimbly up and over. I dropped inside the factory compound and froze on one knee.

All around me were neat, orderly rows of large clay flower bowls, carved spirit houses, horned nugas, and figures in classical dress and pose. They formed a ghostly, miniature army drawn up in ranks and waiting for inspection. Beyond them was the long, tin-roofed factory building where they were made.

It was in darkness, but in one corner of the compound was a small square building I took to be an office, and there a single light burned in a square yellow glow. Someone, I guessed, was making up the books, or counting up the day's takings.

I watched that one pane of light until I was sure that no additional doors or windows were about to open, and then I crossed silently to the darkened main building. I stepped over rows of squat pottery Buddhas, all of them twelve inches high, and then more rows of polished grey elephants.

I found a window that was easily forced with the blade of a knife, and climbed carefully inside. Then I switched on a small, hooded torch and played the slender beam slowly around the pitch black interior of the long factory shed. There were rows of work-benches and tables, and on many of them half-finished examples of the handicrafts I had seen ranged for display outside. There were potter's wheels and shaping tools, and grey canvas smocks hanging from the walls.

I picked my way gingerly between the benches, playing the muffled beam of the torch from one end of the building to the other. I found the kilns where the models were baked, and then the finishing area where they were painted and polished. Finally I found a locked door leading to a more sturdy brick-built extension to the main building. I took out my lock-picking kit and spent a further two minutes in unlocking the door. When the tumblers clicked I turned the handle and moved inside.

The torch beam revealed more finished articles awaiting despatch, a few demon figures, three of the large flower bowls, and a row of four horned *nagas* standing almost thirty inches high. I examined one of the *nagas*, it was fresh and bright and I guessed that the paint was only just dry. I lifted it from the table and found that it was solid and very heavy, not heavy enough for jade or gold, but certainly too heavy for ordinary clay pottery.

There was only one way to prove my theory, and that was to smash away the painted clay shell. There were tools in the factory heavy enough to do the job, or I could have simply hurled the image to the floor. Unfortunately I couldn't adopt either course without leaving positive traces of my visit. I replaced the horned serpent and tested the weight of the three that remained. They were all equally solid and heavy. I moved along the table and was about to examine the first of the flower bowls when I heard a faint sound from outside the factory building.

I couldn't positively identify that sound, but my instinct suggested that it could have been the tentative opening and closing of a door. I listened and it was not repeated, but it was a warning I could not ignore. I began a swift, silent and orderly retreat.

I left the sealed room exactly as I had found it, even sparing the necessary seconds to re-lock the door. I slipped my small wallet with its lock-picking tools back into my inside pocket, and then switched off my torch and plunged the long factory into total darkness. I used both hands to feel my way carefully back between the rows of benches, and relied on the faint bar of starlight to lead me back to the half open window that had given me entry. As I reached it I heard the definite murmur of voices, but for the moment they were on the opposite side of the building.

There was no longer any time to waste. I climbed out of the window, pulled it shut behind me and sprinted for the encircling wall. I needed only a dozen seconds to reach it and disappear into the black night beyond, but I was out of luck. A fiendish sound of barking broke out behind me, and I looked back to see two massive German Wolfhounds come hurtling round the corner of the factory building.

The leading guard dog emitted a

killing howl, and had already launched itself in the final spring that would bring it crashing down on my chest. I saw the white slaver on its snarling jaws and the red fury in its mad eyes. The brute had one solitary thought in its half-size brain, and that was to tear my throat out. For a split second my own brain was petrified by that descending shadow of doom, and yet I reacted with the immediate defensive instinct that I had learned on the judo mats in Sunny Cheong's gymnasium back in Hong Kong. I rolled backwards, my palms smacking hard against the bare earth to alleviate the shock to my spine. As I continued to roll back on to my shoulders my feet came up violently in a thrusting double kick to the Wolfhound's belly. The killing howl turned into an agonized yelp as I hurled the flailing animal clear over my head to go crashing hard into the wall.

I was lucky for instead of landing across rows of the clay figures that could well have broken my back I had rolled neatly between the ranks. I was able to continue my backward somersault and return unshaken to my feet. The second Wolfhound had stopped abruptly in its tracks, its courage faltering as its companion writhed in pain. Then a light and two running figures appeared on the scene. A man shouted and the second dog attacked, but this time I had only three strides to reach the wall.

In those circumstances the six-foot barrier was no barrier at all, and I was straddling the wall in one lightning scramble. I paused to kick the second Wolfhound in its snapping teeth, and as it howled in baffled anger and fell away I heard a familiar voice bellowing angrily behind me.

"That way, Samana — He's on the wall!"

I spared a fleeting glance back. The voice belonged to Gus Rickhardt, and running forward into the light of the lantern Rickhardt carried was a harsh-faced Thai who wore a blue and green sarong and a bright blue headband. Samana was the man who had tried to kill me in the floating market.

I dropped on the safe side of the wall as a heavy automatic banged in the night, and a bullet fired by Rickhardt streaked through the empty space where my head had been silhouetted only a second before.

15

I DIDN'T take the risk of returning directly to Tracey, but first made a long detour to be sure that I had lost all the possibilities of pursuit. Only then did I make my way back to the large mango tree where she waited. As I approached she moved to meet me, and I saw the dim red gleam of her long hair in the starlight. I started to relax, and then my muscles abruptly hardened again as I realized that she was not alone. A second shadow moved out from the gloom beneath the ancient mango, and for a bitter moment I thought that somehow I had been outmanoeuvred by either Rickhardt or Samana.

"Good evening, Mister Chan."

The voice was precise and cultured, and I knew that my first fear was unfounded. However, I was still in trouble, for as he emerged more clearly from the darkness I saw the large black police revolver that was levelled carefully in his right hand.

"Inspector Karachorn!" I tried to match his own smooth smile. "You surprise me again."

"So it would seem." The man was friendly, even if the gun was not. "I trust that your recent escapade has been interesting, perhaps even informative?"

"Towards the end it became rather uncomfortable," I said wryly. Then I looked down at the revolver. "Is that really necessary?"

Karachorn looked down as though he had been temporarily absent-minded. "Forgive me," he apologized, and he returned the weapon to a holster inside his jacket. "I heard a shot only a few minutes ago, and so it seemed prudent to be prepared."

"The shot was fired at me," I informed him.

"I am pleased that it missed, although you do have the unfortunate habit of offering yourself as a target." Karachorn smiled again. "You were investigating the pottery factory, I believe. Miss Ryan and I were just discussing the matter."

"It would be more accurate to say that we were fencing around the subject," Tracey elucidated gently. She looked at me. "The Inspector followed us out from Chieng Mai, David. He saw you climb the factory wall."

Karachorn decided to employ his usual disarming frankness.

"I have kept you all under discreet surveillance," he admitted. "I learned from your taxi driver that today you visited Doy Suthep, and later drove out to the village of Chandi where you returned a jade Buddha to the temple priest. Tonight you make another journey, but instead of calling for a taxi you hired a self-drive car. To me that suggested that perhaps your present movements might be even more incriminating, and so I followed." He regarded me with an open-faced honesty that invited fair speaking in return. "Please, Mister Chan, what did you expect to find at the pottery factory?"

I told him enough to complete the parts of the puzzle that he had already discovered for himself, beginning with the jade Buddha, and the way in which it was involved in the murder of Mark Sanders.

"At the time of the murder I found something that aroused my curiosity," I continued. "In the villa in Hong Kong there was a small workshop that Sanders apparently used for the renovation of some of his art objects, and on the floor of that workshop I found fragments of broken pottery. Nowhere in the workshop, in the villa, or in the two branches of *Exotic Art* that I visited later, could I find any handicrafts shaped in clay pottery. The origin of the broken fragments remained a question, but there was also the question of how did the jade Buddha reach Hong Kong without being intercepted and questioned by customs officials." I paused, and then offered my conclusions:

"I believe, Inspector, that those questions must answer each other. The jade Buddha, and no doubt whole shipments of other smuggled art works, arrived in Hong Kong encased in an outer shell of painted clay pottery. On arrival the shell casings were broken away, and the valuable inner articles removed."

Karachorn nodded slowly, as though he found my hypothesis credible, and so I concluded by bringing the story up to date.

"Mark Sanders received most of his shipments from *Siam Antiquities*, and *Siam Antiquities* buy most of their factory-produced stock here in Chieng Mai. Because the trail led here I followed my instinct and attempted to put my theory to the test."

"And were your suspicions proved?" Karachorn enquired.

Reluctantly I decided that from here it would be expedient to deceive him again.

"I was disturbed before I could learn anything conclusive," I said regretfully. "Two very large guard dogs chased me away."

"And someone fired a shot!"

"That speeded my departure. I didn't look back to see who it might have been."

Karachorn was thoughtful, weighing up what I had told him, and no doubt wondering how much I hadn't told him.

"Why select this particular factory?" he asked.

"Because the others are freely open to tourists, and only this one feels the need for a six-foot protecting wall."

"And guard dogs," Karachorn said wryly. He smiled suddenly and glanced down at his wrist-watch. "The hour is late, Mister Chan, and I have no desire to spend the rest of the night under this mango-tree. Shall we continue this conversation while we walk back to our vehicles?"

★ ★ ★

The white police car was parked immediately behind the small saloon that I had borrowed from the hotel, and I made a mental note of the fact that there was no driver. Karachorn bade us goodnight, and allowed us to precede him on the journey back to Chieng Mai. I drove straight back to the New Oriental, but the headlights of the police car swept past and continued into the centre of the city.

We entered the hotel and I glanced briefly into the bar room. It was almost empty and none of our party were present. I searched further afield and finally found Belinda and Gillian in the television lounge, relaxed in deep armchairs and idly watching some canned variety. They each had a gin and tonic to hand, and Gillian had a positive glow. They looked as though they had spent a calm and comfortable evening.

"Where's Jack?" I enquired.

"He was a little peeved," Belinda said. "I think he had high hopes for tonight and they were all deflated. He went out to drown his sorrows, or something."

"Or something." I repeated blandly.

Tracey gave me an unusually icy look, and so I hastily suggested that we had too earned a drink. Belinda and Gillian held up their glasses for replenishing, and Tracey could only be appeased with a double. I signalled the waiter, and not until we were all seated and served did I embark upon an account of the night's happenings. At the finish I included the facts that I had concealed from Karachorn.

"I didn't see the face of the man who fired the shot and carried the lantern, but I heard his voice and it was unmistakably Gus Rickhardt. And the man he called Samana was the sour-faced Thai with the wrinkles who tried to blast me with that Armalite rifle."

"So we are on the right track," Belinda observed softly. "But did you find anything that would prove it?"

I nodded, and described the four horned serpents I had found in the locked room. "Look at any temple in Thailand," I reminded her, "And you'll find that every corner of every roof is adorned with one of those images. That architectural style has persisted for hundreds of years, and I'm positive that if I had broken away those pottery shells tonight then underneath I would have found genuine *nagas* in the original stone — the *naga* images that have been broken from the roofs of the ruined temples which we know have been looted in the jungles."

"That would explain how the smaller items are smuggled out of the country." Tracey agreed. "But what about the bigger stuff? You've said that these people will strip a location of practically every stone, and they wouldn't be able to disguise a whole wall or a doorway as a pottery imitation of the real thing."

"They would need another method for the really heavy pieces," Belinda said. "And the usual method would be to ship them out in crates marked as agricultural machinery, or something similar. But I think David could be right about the smaller stuff. Smaller intact pieces are more valuable, and to the gang concerned it would be worth the extra effort and care to ensure that they could stand up to a routine customs examination as modern-produced handicrafts."

There was a moment of contemplative silence, and then Tracey gave me a straight look.

"David, why did you keep so much of this back from Karachorn?"

"Because I'm not yet certain of his motives," I said quietly. "I don't doubt his identity, but our Bangkok Police Inspector plays too much of a lone hand. When he first appeared I thought it strange that he didn't bring the usual sergeant along to provide support and take notes. Now he follows us to Chieng Mai, when he could just as easily have notified the local police and put in a request for them to keep a track of all our movements. Also tonight he chose to calmly ignore the fact that I had taken the law into my own hands by breaking and entering into private property. He could have had me arrested for that, but he didn't." I paused, but I could think of no better way to define my feelings and finished, "Karachorn is taking too personal an interest in this case, and one which I suspect is not entirely official."

"There is such a thing as a bent cop," Tracey suggested.

"Or a cop who is over-dedicated." Belinda was more generous. "David said that in Bangkok Karachorn appeared to be obsessed with a genuine anger towards these temple thieves. Perhaps he is waging a private war, and turning a blind eye to some of our activities because he hopes that we will eventually lead him to the gang he's after."

I couldn't disagree with either of them.

"For the moment," I said, "We'll reserve judgement."

* * *

It was late, and so we broke up the conversation and retired. I bade goodnight to Belinda and Tracey at their door, and then escorted Gillian round the corner of the corridor to her own room. She hesitated on the threshold, and then said in a low voice,

"David, can I talk to you alone?"

She suddenly looked unhappy, and so after a moment's hesitation I followed her inside and closed the door. Before I could switch on the light she pressed herself against me and put her arms round my waist. Her mouth was muffled against my chest as she said miserably,

"I've been a fool, haven't I, David? You found those pieces of broken pottery in my father's workshop. That means that he must have broken the shell away from the jade Buddha — so he must have known that the Buddha was stolen. I've been deceiving myself all the time."

I put one arm around her shoulders, and with the other hand I gently lifted her face and made her look up into my eyes. I could see the tear trails on her cheeks, and said quietly,

"Perhaps he did know, but that doesn't necessarily make him bad. He probably thought that it was just another relic that had been dug up from a lost ruin, something valuable, but something that no one would ever miss because no one had even known that it was there. I'm sure he didn't know all the real details."

Gillian stared at me hopefully, and then accepted that ray of comfort. However she kept her arms around me, and I guessed that too many gins and tonic had tangled her emotions I held her quietly, not wanting to take advantage, or to reject her, and found myself wondering about her future.

"What will you do when all this is over?" I asked.

She was silent for another minute, but then decided to answer. Her small, lost face looked up at me again in the darkness.

"I shall go back to England, I suppose. I wouldn't really feel at home in Hong Kong, and I could never live in the villa now. All my friends are in England, and I have some relatives there. I'll probably get a flat and a job in London."

I nodded my approval, for she would have to make her own life somewhere. She smiled suddenly and asked:

"Have you ever been to London, David?"

I nodded again. "Like you I was educated in an English Public School, although I imagine that I was less acceptable than you."

She looked intrigued. "What do you mean?"

"I mean that I'm Eurasian, but my father wasn't the conventional lonely army officer amusing himself with a Chinese wife. Instead my mother was a highly unconventional officer's daughter, who had plenty of choice, yet chose to fall in love with a very remarkable Chinese." I smiled. "For some inexplicable reason that reversal of the usual marital arrangement wasn't considered all so jolly and sporting by my conservative classmates."

She laughed. "They must have been snobs. Did you care?"

"Perhaps, but not now." I smiled again. "It induced me to return to Hong Kong where I now have a thriving detective agency, not to mention two glamorous partners."

That made her thoughtful, and the gins and tonic had made her as bold as she was curious.

"Do you sleep with Belinda or Tracey?" she asked bluntly.

I had to make a positive effort to haul my bland expression into place.

"Sleeping with someone has to be very brief or very permanent," I explained. "Anything in between tends to end with some degree of heartbreak."

That seemed to satisfy her, for she held me more tightly and her voice became thick and husky with a desiring fear.

"David, would you sleep with me?"

She sensed my hesitation and rushed on quickly, "David, please don't tell me that I'm too young. I'm a woman of eighteen, and this is supposed to be a permissive age! At school I was the only virgin in my class!"

"The others were only trying to impress you," I said. "They were probably all virgins too. In any case, perhaps it's something you shouldn't throw away."

"I'm not throwing it away." She kissed me passionately. "I want to give it to you. I'm only a virgin because I didn't want to throw it away on some clumsy boy who only half knew what he was doing. I want my first time to be with a man who knows it all."

She had a valid argument, and she was sweet and she was persistent, so finally I taught her gently all that she needed to know.

16

I APPEARED in the dining room the next morning only five minutes late for breakfast. Belinda and Tracey were already seated at the table, and tackling large orders of eggs and bacon with a refined gusto that would have made the average woman fretting about her calories turn green with envy. It always amazed me that they could serve such healthy appetites without doing any damage to those voluptuous curves, although they did maintain that it was the constant exercise and effort involved in keeping me out of trouble that kept their classic statistics in such shapely trim. They smiled me a joint welcome, and Belinda paused to enquire,

"What's happened to Gillian this morning?"

Gillian was sleeping soundly, and, I hoped, dreaming happily. Those had been her professed intentions when I had left her in a state of blissful exhaustion an hour earlier. However, I called up my most inscrutable expression and answered blandly,

"You may have given her too many gins and tonic last night. She's probably got a hangover."

Belinda gave me her cool, mind-reading look, her hazel eyes faintly doubtful behind the elegant golden butterfly frames of her spectacles, but then Jack Holden arrived and forestalled any further questions on that topic. He sat down heavily and his attitude was a degree less friendly than before. He nodded briefly to the girls and then aimed his grey eyes at mine.

"Where did you go last night?" he demanded.

I had given a great amount of thought to the subject of exactly how much I should enlighten Jack Holden, but I decided to fence around the issue first.

"I had an idea that I thought was

worth checking out." I smiled him an apology. "I'm sorry that I needed Tracey's help."

"Why take Tracey, we had a date. Why couldn't Belinda give you the help you needed?"

"Because Tracey knew the way — Belinda didn't."

"The way to where, for Christ's sake?"

He was showing severe irritation and his approach was perfect. Either he was angry because I had persuaded Tracey to break off their dinner arrangement, or he was angry because I had been investigating behind his back and he was covering neatly. I wondered how much he already knew, remembering that he too had been absent for most of last night.

"I was interested in the pottery village you showed Tracey yesterday afternoon." I pretended that the information was imparted with some reluctance. "She pointed out the factories to me."

Holden looked baffled. "Why go back there at night? What's so special about a village that makes pottery?"

I hesitated, and then told him all that I had decided he should know.

"I had a theory, Jack, connected with that jade Buddha I returned to Chandi. After Mark Sanders was murdered I found some pottery fragments on the floor of his workshop. They made me believe that the jade Buddha had been smuggled into Hong Kong inside a pottery shell. I've been looking for an opportunity to check that theory ever since we arrived in Thailand. Yesterday when Tracey told me that each little village around here specializes in its own handicraft industry, and that one of those villages was devoted solely to making articles in pottery, I decided to play my hunch."

"You mean you went prowling around those pottery factories at night?"

"Only one of them. I by-passed those that were wide-open to visiting tourists. I concentrated on the one factory that had felt it necessary to build a six-foot wall to keep out intruders."

Holden's anger was evaporating, and he was becoming curious.

"Did you find anything?"

"Yes and no," I said ruefully. "I didn't learn anything about the factory itself because it was too well guarded. I managed to get into the building, but I was disturbed almost immediately and had to get out fast. Someone set a couple of German Wolfhounds on to me, and I only just got back over the wall in time."

I paused, giving him time to prompt me. He didn't, he simply stared into my face. Finally I went on:

"While I was on the wall I heard someone shout. I looked back and saw two men run round the corner of the factory building. One carried a lantern, and he was the one who shouted. He called the second man by name, something like Samana." Again I paused, and again Holden simply waited. "Samana was a Thai with a harsh, wrinkled face. And he wore the same blue and green sarong, and the same blue headband, that he wore when he tried to kill me from that passing speedboat on the floating market. This time, luckily for me, he didn't have his Armalite rifle with him. His friend had an automatic, but they're not so reliable at a distance. He fired one shot and missed."

"Who was the second man?" Holden asked.

"I don't know," I lied with a straight face. "He was behind the lantern. I only recognized the man he called Samana because Samana ran forward into the light. With two dogs and a bullet hunting for my heels I didn't stop to see any more."

Holden looked to Tracey, but she merely shrugged.

"David left me to wait well away from the factory. I heard the dogs barking and the shot, and I was very relieved when he re-appeared several minutes later."

Holden frowned, and then looked back at me.

"If you're sure about this man Samana, then it means that you must be on the right track," he said slowly.

"It's an indication, but it's no proof," I said regretfully. "The guard dogs, the surrounding wall, and the fact that someone was ready to shoot at any stray intruders, are all indications that that particular factory is involved in something less innocent than the mere manufacture of pottery handicrafts. Unfortunately none of it is positive proof, and if Samana disappears then there is only my word that he was ever there. In fact there's only my word that a shot was fired. Tracey only heard the muffled echoes from a distance."

"So why the hell didn't you let me know what you were planning last night?" Holden spoke with exasperation. "I thought that I was supposed to be helping on this case, not just stooging along for the ride. I could have come along with you last night. With two of us we might have been able to tackle Mister Samana and his friend. In any case it wouldn't be just your word that you'd recognized his face, it would be our word. Maybe we could have gone to the police this morning and got them interested?" He banged a fist on the table and repeated: "Hell, David — why didn't you tell me some of this in advance?"

"I'm sorry about that." I made every effort to sound sincere. "I suppose it's a bad habit of mine to play a lone hand. Belinda and Tracey will follow me anywhere, but the last thing I want is to expose either of them to any unnecessary danger. That means that when I do have to take chances I tend to do the job first, and then enlighten them afterwards. Last night I simply complied with my usual practice."

Holden looked as though he wasn't quite fooled by my bland assurance, but then Belinda smiled at him and said wryly,

"I told you last night that he wouldn't

tell me exactly what he was up to — and I'll bet Tracey didn't know either until the last minute."

Tracey supported her with an affirmative nod, and so Holden was obliged to accept the matter at face value. I didn't want him smarting internally from any imagined slight, so I was quick to ask his advice.

"Jack, how well do you know that particular pottery factory?"

"You said it was the factory with the six-foot wall — that means it's the one on the right as you drive through the village?"

"That's the one."

"I don't." He shrugged. "I've placed orders with two of those factories, but I've never done business with that particular firm."

"Even so, there's no reason why you shouldn't do business there. As a buyer for *Siam Antiquities* you would have a legitimate reason for paying them a visit."

"I suppose so. I could always

compare prices, or look for original lines." He rubbed his jaw thoughtfully. "Are you suggesting that I should do something like that, and at the same time give the place a good look over?"

I nodded. "There's a chance that you might learn something. I'm sure that no one recognized me last night, so they may not be unduly alarmed." I paused and added a morsel of bait. "Tracey never went within half a mile of the place, so it should be perfectly safe for her to go with you."

Holden thought about it. "If we waste time it's only a couple of hours." He looked at Tracey and she nodded in agreement. "Okay," he finished. "We'll go out there this morning."

★ ★ ★

After they had gone I remained at the breakfast table, alone with Belinda. She stirred her second cup of coffee slowly while I did justice to my scrambled eggs, grilled tomatoes and toast, and finally she said gently,

"You didn't tell Jack that you found those four *nagas* in that locked room — or that you recognized Gus Rickhardt — or about your meeting with Karachorn. You gave him only half the story at the most."

I hadn't realized until then how hungry I was, and I stopped eating with reluctance.

"The half that I suspect he already knows," I admitted.

"And you're still hoping that given enough rope he will obligingly hang himself."

I nodded. "If Holden does have any connection with Rickhardt, then Rickhardt will soon know all that I've confided to Holden, and then we can expect some positive moves."

"Meaning Samana?" Belinda queried gravely. "You were not exactly subtle when you hinted that it would be convenient for the other side if Samana were to disappear."

"Not subtle enough for my clever Belinda," I complimented her. "But I have hopes that I may have sown the intended thought in the mind of Jack Holden. If our Thai friend with the wrinkled face turns up as a corpse in some dark corner, then we shall know that Holden has informed Rickhardt that Samana is a source of danger to their operation."

"That's rather hard on Samana."

"I haven't forgotten that he made a very determined attempt to kill me." I smiled grimly. "In the circumstances I am not at all averse to the thought of putting his particular head on the chopping block."

"And if Jack isn't a villain?" Belinda smiled. "It is possible you know, despite his designs on Tracey. And he did make the un-villain-like suggestion that if he had been with you last night then you could both have gone to the police this morning."

"I think Jack was fairly confident that I wouldn't go to the police at this early stage." I smiled in turn and added, "But I haven't entirely been neglecting the other possibilities. So far we have five suspects for Mark Sander's murder." I ticked them off on the fingers of one hand. "First there's the young Thai who fled from the villa, who may or may not be connected with Samana and Rickhardt. Second and third we have Holden and Srivaji, either of whom could have been double-crossing Mark Sanders, or could have been double-crossed by Mark Sanders. There are enough twists and tangles in their combined business relationships for anything to be possible. Then of course there is Gus Rickhardt, whose role is still uncertain."

"So how do you propose to sort them out?"

"I'm hoping that your personal charm and influence can work even at a distance," I said blandly. "We know that one of those four was in Hong Kong at the time of the murder. What I want to know is whether any of the other three were also in Hong Kong at that time. I'd like you to cable Superintendent Davies with complete descriptions of Rickhardt, Holden and Srivaji, and ask him if he can compare them with the lists of passengers who flew in and out of Hong Kong around the time that Sanders was killed."

"I'll send the cable for you, and I'm sure that on this case Ray will co-operate." Belinda paused. "But originally you mentioned five suspects, and you've only listed four."

"I haven't forgotten your warning about Gillian," I said quietly. "I hope you're wrong, but I haven't forgotten."

★ ★ ★

The rest of the day passed slowly. Tracey and Holden returned shortly after noon with a negative report. They had been conducted on an open tour of the pottery factory, and to justify their interest Holden had placed an order on behalf of *Siam Antiquities*.

However, they had seen nothing out of the ordinary to arouse their suspicions. It was the report I had expected them to bring, and so I merely shrugged patiently and said that now we could only wait.

"Wait what for?" Holden demanded.

"For chance to lead the man called Samana across our path again," I said blandly. "He's our best lead now, and we know that he is here in Chieng Mai."

★ ★ ★

We spent the afternoon strolling around the streets and temples of Thailand's northern capital, ostensibly searching for that hoped-for glimpse of a blue headband and a blue and green sarong. Tracey and Holden took one direction, while Belinda and Gillian and I took another. We met again at the New Oriental with nothing to report, and Holden looked somewhat frustrated with my vague assertions that there was nothing much that we could do except to continue to search and wait until we did find the tracks of our quarry.

It was Gillian who pointed out that an exhibition programme of Thai classical dancing was being staged in the hotel that night. She wanted to watch, and as there was no reason to deny her the pleasure we reserved seats. Holden seemed uncertain whether he should attempt to steer Tracey away from the main party again, but finally decided that they would join us.

Dinner was again a pleasure, the food, the wine, and the gay company of the girls in delightfully low-cut evening dresses being all that any man could demand. Gillian gave me loving looks, and I realized almost with a sense of guilt that the shy schoolgirl in the blue mini skirt had gone for ever, and in her place was an accomplished young woman with a full knowledge of her sexual power.

The cabaret was staged in the dining

room, and after the meal we pulled our chairs round to one side of the table to watch. For this particular evening all the tables around us are fully occupied, but Gillian was unconcerned. As the lights dimmed she leaned her head confidently on my shoulder.

The dancing began, accompanied by a slow, tinkling rhythm played on drums and xylophone. From the darkened wings six smiling young Thai girls moved gracefully into the spotlight in the centre of the stage. They wore costumes of dazzling brilliance, in red, purple, blue, green, gold and silver, while their headpieces were delicate, golden pagoda spires. Their dance was a symbolic gesture of welcome, the steps dainty, and performed with a gentle, fluid swaying movement of the body. All expression was in their arms, hands and fingers, tracing exquisite patterns in the air.

Gillian snuggled closer to me, entranced and happy. The dance ended when the six girls gently showered lotus petals on the front ranks of the watching guests, and I saw Holden move quickly to secure a flower for Tracey.

The second part of the programme involved twelve dancers, which meant double the movement, double the grace, and double the colour. I found myself fascinated, and began to relax to the strange, tinkling music. Every subtle gesture was so gentle yet full of meaning that it was almost possible to be hypnotized by the slowly weaving dancers.

The contrast came suddenly with the leaping appearance of two male dancers, one in a costume of spangled black, and the other in spangled white. The black dancer wore a hideous demon mask, while the white dancer had the addition of a long, curling tail, and wore the equally grotesque mask of a monkey. They carried sticks which they rattled furiously in mock sword-play. While they fought Holden leaned to one side and offered a brief explanation of the story.

"They're acting out a scene from the Ramayana," he whispered. "This is the battle between Hanuman the Monkey General, and Ravan the Demon King."

As Holden spoke the dancers clashed and then sprang apart. The music struck a high note and vibrated with great intensity, and the white dancer twirled on one heel and crouched to face our table. Behind the gross parody of the monkey mask I saw two human eyes blazing fiercely, and from the seemingly harmless stick in his hands I saw the sudden flash of genuine steel as the hidden blade was withdrawn.

In that same split second the lights went out.

17

THE sudden shock of darkness was absolute, but I had seen enough of that emerging sliver of steel to be warned. Gillian had pulled away from me to hear Holden's murmured account of what the plot entailed, and so I was free to duck swiftly in the opposite direction. I sensed the vicious movement as the monkey dancer lunged forward, and heard the hiss of the blade plucking at my sleeve. The impact as the needle point drove home into the back of my chair almost tilted the chair over backwards with my weight still on the seat. In the blackness my right hand found the smooth curve of Belinda's thigh and I used it as a lever to push myself forward. Belinda's startled, and faintly indignant gasp, the crash of my overturning chair and Gillian's scream all sounded in the same moment.

Then the lights came on again.

I saw the long black tail of the monkey dancer bobbing out of sight behind the curtain to the left of the stage. However, Gillian's scream cost me a second as I glanced back. She was unhurt, but staring down in horror at my collapsed chair with a two foot rapier impaled neatly in the dead centre of the chair back. The restaurant was full of horrified faces, and another woman screamed and fainted.

I lost no more time and plunged in pursuit. The Demon King and the Monkey General had both vanished, but that fleeting glimpse of a tail had shown me the direction in which to follow. I ran across the stage in turn and thrust through the curtains.

A group of girl dancers stood there, startled and alarmed, their white-painted faces now looking hollow with fear, and highlighted horrifically by their gorgeously coloured and spangled costumes. They were incapable of speech, but there was only one exit and I went through the only doorway without a pause. A short corridor brought me bursting into the kitchens where a collection of equally startled cook boys and kitchen maids gaped at me with pop eyes and open mouths. My gaze swept the whole area in this space of seconds and again I saw that black tail disappearing through a doorway on the far side.

I heard footsteps behind me, a ring of fleet high heels that suggested Belinda and Tracey but I didn't look back. I vaulted over a long steel-topped table littered with chopping knives and vegetables and continued the chase. A cook boy dropped a saucepan and somewhere crockery crashed as a maid stumbled away in panic. Shouts, howls and pandemonium suddenly raged but by then I was through and leaving it all behind.

I emerged into the gardens behind the hotel and saw two shadowy figures racing ahead. The white spangles of the

Monkey General's costume made him an easy target to follow through the night, although the Demon King was already merging into blackness. The gate that led out from the gardens into the street was unlocked and open and they both darted through.

By this time I was certain that I knew the identity of the man in the monkey mask. His general height and build, his speed of movement, and the agility with which he had performed in the dance and afterwards wcre all positive clues. This was our third encounter, and although he had escaped me in Hong Kong, and again in the floating markets of Bangkok, I was determined that this time he must not get away. There were too many questions that only he could answer, and I put on a scorching burst of speed to follow him through the gardens and the gate.

At the back of the hotel flowed the lazy, winding course of the Mae Ping River, and the two fugitives in their grotesque dance costumes were racing madly along the road that ran parallel to the river. They had turned away from the centre of Chieng Mai and were heading for the safer darkness beyond the suburbs. They had a thirty yard start but I lengthened my stride and concentrated every effort into closing the gap. For the first hundred yards they maintained their lead, but this time I had the advantage. In that spangled white costume the Monkey General had no hope of losing me in the darkness. Also he and his companion had expended a large amount of energy in the vigorous mock battle they had performed in the dance scene from the Ramayana. He had proved my match before, but this time I was starting fresh and without a constricting monkey suit. The balance was tipped in my favour and slowly I began to overhaul him on the second hundred yards.

At five hundred yards I was almost within reach of that bobbing black tail. The Monkey General was faltering and I could hear him panting for breath inside the heavy mask that fitted over his head and shoulders. The waving tail attached to his backside made a ridiculous and elusive target. Three times I made the extra effort to lunge forward and three times it evaded my grasp. On the fourth try my fist closed in a firm grip and I yanked hard. The tail ripped away in my hand, but the jerk was enough to tumble the Monkey General off his feet. He lost his balance and fell down a pitch dark slope towards the river.

I plunged after him on the slope of waste ground that was littered with discarded rubbish and small bushes. Our bodies collided heavily as he tried to get up and I made a fast effort to get a half nelson lock around his neck. The bulky monkey mask made the move impossible and left me vulnerable to a savage elbow drive into the stomach as he wriggled round easily in my grasp. The contorted monkey face was grinning into mine and the human eyes behind it blazed with dark fury. His knee was coming up for my crotch, but I dropped away from it and down, and succeeded in clamping on a leg hold that enabled me to hurl him heavily over on to his back.

For a moment we wrestled violently, and then he used his free leg to lash out a violent heel kick at the side of my head. If he had been wearing hard shoes the kick would have knocked me senseless, and even with his soft dancing shoes the blow was enough to dislodge me from my hold. A series of bells rang dizzily in my head as I reeled away, but I sensed that he was scrambling to his feet and so I did the same.

We faced each other, panting hoarsely in the night. The Monkey General suddenly resorted to his favourite method of boxing footwork and leaped into another attack. I blocked his lashing foot and responded with a high kick of my own. He half turned to avoid it but the sole of my foot thudded into his shoulder. He spun off balance and sprawled full length, and this time the monkey mask rolled off his shoulders and bounced like a misshapen football until it splashed noisily into the river. My opponent hauled himself up into a crouch, and then looked to face me. The last shadow of doubt was gone, for the face revealed was that of the handsome young Thai from the villa.

I waited for him, ready to continue the fight, but while he struggled up I was able to speak for the first time.

"This is our third meeting," I said hoarsely. "Isn't it time we stopped fighting and began talking."

I didn't get an answer because we were no longer alone. I heard Tracey shout, and spun round to see that the black dancer in the costume of the Demon King had also reappeared to find his companion. The starlight glinted on the sharp blade of the knife in his hand and he rushed at me like the avenging demon he was supposed to be. I pivoted on my heel to meet him, but then something dark which

I later recognized as Tracey's handbag hurtled over my shoulder. The sharp corner of the handbag struck heavily against the ferocious demon mask and knocked it sideways. The black dancer blundered to a halt, suddenly blind and missing his target. I closed with him swiftly, driving a solid punch to his lower belly to deflate him completely, and then wrestling the knife from his grasp.

As the black dancer dropped at my feet I heard the young Thai in the white monkey suit lurching forward to renew his attack. I wheeled again to face him, the knife now slicing a threatening arc in my own hand. The young Thai hesitated, as though even now he might be prepared to risk the blade, and then Belinda's voice rang out sharp and clear from the edge of the waste ground.

"Stop it!" She commanded. "If there is any more fighting I will shoot!"

We both turned to face the sound. Her dark figure was standing in shadow under a clump of trees, and her outstretched hand gripped something squat and black that was pointed ominously in our direction. Her stance and voice were so completely in control of the situation that the young Thai had no doubt that she was pointing a gun. His hands slumped down to his sides in a gesture of surrender.

There was a moment of silence while we all regained our breath. Then the black dancer on the ground began to groan and pushed himself up into a sitting position. He struggled to remove his twisted demon face mask, and the white dancer moved to help him. The two girls remained on the edge of the waste ground, Belinda still poised in her threatening position in the shadows, and Tracey standing on one foot and leaning rather heavily against a tree. I couldn't spare them much attention because I was watching the two young Thais. The monkey dancer stared back at me with cold eyes.

"For a start we could exchange

names," I suggested. "Mine is David Chan — who are you?"

For a moment it seemed that I was to meet with nothing except a hostile silence, then the Monkey General spoke.

"I am Anandha. This is my brother Kueno."

"Why did you try to kill me, Anandha?"

That question brought an immediate and bitter response.

"Because you are one of the evil ones who stole the Chandi Buddha."

"No," I denied the charge quietly. "Until the night we fought in Hong Kong I had never seen the Chandi Buddha. I am a private detective, a kind of private policeman, and since that night I have been trying to return the Chandi Buddha, and to find the evil ones you mentioned."

He glowered at me with obvious disbelief, and so I tried another question.

"Why is the Chandi Buddha so

important to you? Are you a monk?"

"No." The bitterness flowed back into the one word.

"Then what?"

His lips tightened, and he glanced briefly at his brother who now sat silently at his feet. Finally he spoke again:

"Once," he said bleakly, "There were three brothers."

I had a sudden flash of intuition, one of those rare moments of insight that only comes when one is in any case within a split second of the truth.

"Once there were three brothers," I repeated softly. "They were Anandha, and Keuno — and Muang?"

I had hit the mark exactly. Anandha and Koenu both became rigid, and their eyes were black with grief and hate. Kueno started to rise, but Anandha held him back.

"So you know the name of Muang," the older brother challenged grimly. "That means that you must be one of the evil ones who took his life."

"No," I said quietly, for I could see the killing fury burning again in his eyes. I had to stop his forward movement with another question.

"Would the temple thieves fleeing from their crime stop to learn the name of the boy they had murdered?"

Anandha hesitated. "Then how did you learn the name of Muang?"

"Yesterday when I returned the jade Buddha to the village of Chandi. The Learned Bhikkhu there was grateful to see the image replaced on his altar. He told me the story of how the temple was robbed in the night, and how the thieves murdered the boy monk Muang to stop him raising the alarm."

Anandha and Kueno exchanged doubting glances, and I realized that the moment had come to win their trust. I reversed the blade of the knife I had taken from Kueno, and offered it to Anandha hilt first.

"Take this," I said. "For I do not believe that we are enemies."

Anandha took the knife slowly, and

then looked to the dark patch of shadow where Belinda still waited.

"Belinda," I said quietly, "Come here and show our friends the gun in your hand."

Belinda walked calmly towards us, and as she approached it became slowly obvious that the object in her right hand was not quite the right shape for an automatic. She opened her hand and offered it to Anandha, and all that lay in her palm was the harmless black case that housed her spare pair of spectacles. For a moment the two brothers stared, and then Anandha began to laugh.

While we relaxed Tracey retrieved her handbag, and I noticed that she was limping badly. She came to join us, but there was still no time to ascertain what damage she had done. Before the smiling mood could pass away I asked Anandha to explain all that he had been trying to achieve.

"The return of the Chandi Buddha," he answered. "And vengeance for our brother Muang."

"How were you able to follow the Chandi Buddha to Hong Kong?"

"It was not difficult. My brother Kueno worked at the pottery village. He recognized the shape of the Chandi Buddha after it had been encased in a pottery shell. He saw the ugly American prepare the Buddha for despatch with a shipment of other articles, and although he had no chance to steal back the Buddha he wrote down the address to which the shipment was being sent. The name he wrote down was Mark Sanders, and the address was the *Exotic Art* shop in Hong Kong. We decided that I should go to Hong Kong, and find this man Sanders, and bring back the Chandi Buddha."

I nodded slowly, using my intuition to fill in the gaps in his story. If Kueno had worked at the pottery factory then obviously he would have been previously aware of the smuggling racket in which the factory was involved. No doubt the moral ethics of the business had not particularly concerned him, until the younger brother had been killed. Then for the two surviving brothers it had become a personal vendetta which they could not take to the police.

"You went to Hong Kong alone?" I asked.

Anandha nodded. "Kueno does not speak English, so it seemed best that he remained behind."

"So it was you who killed Mark Sanders."

Anandha shook his head. "No, I found out where he lived and went to the villa, but I did not kill him." He smiled bleakly. "If the man Sanders had been alive I might have killed him, but he was already dead. I looked at his body, and then I looked carefully through the house. I touched nothing until I found a small workshop where the Chandi Buddha was standing on the table. It was still encased in the pottery shell. I broke the pottery casing away, and then I left the house. I saw you arrive with a young girl, and I crouched in some bushes. When I tried to escape from the garden you gave chase — " Disgust filtered into his tone as he concluded, "And I lost the Chandi Buddha."

"So you came back to Thailand," I prompted him gently. "I chased you again in the floating market at Bangkok. Why were you there?"

Anandha shrugged. "I had failed to bring back the Buddha, but still I wanted vengeance for our brother Muang. Kueno knew that when genuine objects were concealed in pottery they were always sent to only two places. The first was *Exotic Art* in Hong Kong, and the other was to Mister Srivaji of *Siam Antiquities* in Bangkok. I wanted to find out more about this Mister Srivaji."

"Did you learn anything?"

Anandha shrugged again, a negative gesture without words.

"What about the American Jack Holden? Do you know anything about him?"

"Nothing." Anandha moved his shoulders for the third time.

"The other American, Gus Rickhardt?" I persisted. He still looked blank so I added a description. "The ugly American with the broken teeth?"

"That one!" Anandha spat. "That one is the boss of the gang that robs the temples. The others are bad Thai men, and their boss is the man Samana, but the biggest boss is the ugly American. We believe that it was he who killed our brother Muang."

"Do you know where Samana and the ugly American are to be found now?"

Anandah nodded. "North of here there is a ruined temple in the jungle. Even now the temple robbers are pulling down the walls and digging up the earth. Kueno and I have watched them, but they are many and they all have rifles. We have not yet got close enough to kill the ugly American."

I remembered the old priest of Chandi pointing towards the ruins he claimed lay to the west of his village, and guessed that this must be the same location.

"Can you take me there?" I asked quietly. "I too would like to witness these temple robbers at their work."

Anandha gave me a hard look. I had demanded too many answers and given him no opportunity to ask any questions of his own. Now suspicion crept obliquely into his voice.

"How do I know that I can trust you?"

"That is a fair question," I acknowledged. "If you wish I will accompany you to the village of Chandi, and there you can speak with the temple priest. He will be able to show you the jade Buddha back in its rightful place. Will that be the proof you need?"

Anandha continued to stare into my eyes for another half minute, but then he was satisfied. He nodded briefly.

"I will believe you, David Chan. We will waste time to go first to Chandi, and so I will lead you direct to the secret place of the ruins. Only remember that the jungle is a dangerous place at night, and that these men we seek are even more deadly than the black cobras that will lie in wait in the darkness."

18

IT was obvious that the girls could not accompany us, for at the tail end of the chase Tracey had fallen badly and twisted her ankle. She had crawled to the edge of the battleground only just in time to hurl her handbag at Kueno, but now she could barely walk and needed Belinda's shoulder to help her stand upright. Bravely Tracey insisted that she could limp back to the hotel alone, giving Belinda the opportunity to protest that there was no reason why she should not be allowed to share the remainder of the night's events. However, I believed in Anandha's dire warnings, and I wanted both my girls to stay safely out of range of both cobras and killers with rifles.

"Someone has to stall Jack Holden," I said weakly, "And it may need all your combined charms." I paused.

"Incidentally, what happened to Jack?"

"He stopped for Gillian," Belinda said. "She had a sudden burst of hysterics. Then I should imagine that he was caught up with the manager and his staff, they were all converging on the excitement when I left." She smiled. "I only just got clear. After the rest of you had all dashed through the kitchen the cook boys got brave and tried to hold me back. I had to throw one poor little man into a corner."

"Tell him you're sorry on the way back," I suggested. "After all, we did create chaos in his kitchen."

"And what do we tell Jack?" Tracey demanded.

"Something simple." I thought about it. "Just tell him that you lost all of us in the night. Your lame ankle is a perfect excuse for giving up the chase, and Belinda stopped to help you. Holden will be making his own guesses anyway, and pleading ignorance is your easiest way out."

They gave me troubled looks and

then Belinda said slowly, "Alright, David, but watch out for those snakes."

I knew she meant the human as well as the sinuous variety, and I nodded my assurance. In response to the concern in her eyes I kissed her briefly. Then I kissed Tracey. For me it was impossible to choose between them, but together they had the sweetest lips that I had ever known. They turned away, and I was alone with Kueno and Anandha.

"How can we get within striking distance of these ruins?" I asked. "Do you have a car?"

"No." Anandha showed his teeth in a faint smile. "But we do have very good Japanese motor cycles!"

★ ★ ★

Their machines were two 175cc Sazukis which were carefully hidden behind a large clump of bushes further along the road. The two brothers wheeled their bikes out into the open, and then paused only to strip off their spangled dance costumes which they stuffed into saddle bags. Underneath they wore shorts and vests, and with the addition of light weight zip-up jackets and the two spaceman-type helmets that hung from the handlebars they were ready to go. I let them mount and kick-start the bikes, and then climbed on to the pillion seat behind Anandha. The bikes roared as the throttles were wound open simultaneously, and with a swift, racing gear change we were on our way.

We skirted Chieng Mai, and headed out on to the north road that led towards Chandi. The double weight proved only a slight handicap to Anandha's machine, but allowed Kueno to lead the way. The wind sang in my ears, and as the road bumped up into the northern foothills it became an exhilarating ride. The popular Japanese machines, although small, were fast and sturdy, and we were modern knights of bushido riding steel ponies behind lances of light. Anandha and Kueno were familiar with the road, and for them darkness meant no reduction of speed. They rode with skill and confidence, which I quickly began to share.

The black, jungle hills closed in on the twisting course of the road, rushing past on either side in a blur of darkness. Above hung the stars in a brilliant map of the heavens, and ahead the two flickering headlight beams picked out glimpses of undergrowth and forest, and once a pair of baleful eyes staring back from the edge of the road. The tarmac surface became narrower and more pitted, and the Sazuki began to bounce more erratically. I took a firmer grip with my knees and clamped my hand on to Anandha's hunched shoulder to prevent myself from being left behind.

After three-quarters of an hour the ride ended, when I judged that we were still a few miles short of the village of Chandi. The stop light on Kueno's machine glowed red as he braked, and Anandha skidded to a flourishing halt beside him. They closed down the throttles and switched off their engines, and then Anandha looked back over his shoulder.

"From here we must enter the jungle," he advised me. "The road can take us no closer."

I eased myself off the pillion and thankfully straightened my back. The two Thais quickly dismounted and pushed the motor cycles a few yards into the trees. There they switched off the lights, and satisfied that their machines were again well hidden they returned to the road. They had left their space helmets behind, and gazed at me with serious eyes.

"There is a path," Anandha said. "It is used by hunters from the hill tribes who track game for food. It leads to the far ridges, and beyond that to the mountains of Burma-land, but it passes close to the secret place of the ruins."

"Let us follow the path," I answered.

Anandha nodded and led the way.

I followed, and Kueno trotted on my heels.

As we entered the forest the star map of the heavens was blotted out, and we were enveloped in total but living darkness. Every unseen leaf and branch brushed and clawed at our faces, and beyond our own clumsy crashing there was the constant rustling and whisper of jungle sound. The nocturnal movements of every small mammal and rodent were magnified beyond all proportion, and yet were almost lost in the overall buzz of insect activity and the clicking whir of invisible crickets. It was a blind world, full of menace.

"Tread heavily," Anandha advised, "So that the snakes may feel the vibrations of our approach and have time to move away. If you step on one it will strike."

I had been endeavouring to walk silently, but his words made sense and from that point on I stamped down hard with every stride. I kept my left hand clamped on his shoulder, and in turn I felt Kueno's hand repeatedly touching my sleeve. I could see nothing in that all-enveloping blackness, and I could only trust to Anandha's sense of direction. I guessed that our hunter's path must be the only possible way of making progress, and that consequently Anandha was simply following the only course that offered no resistance. If he had strayed off the path we would have come to a dead stop in the tangle of undergrowth and vines on either side.

We moved at a cautious pace, frequently tripping over an ill-placed root, or slipping on the carpet of wet leaves under-foot. Once we blundered into what seemed like an impassable thicket of bamboos, but Anandha turned unhesitatingly to the right and worked his way around it. In the pitch blackness, with strange noises in my ears and damp, rotting smells assailing my nostrils, my imagination began to run riot. I could almost feel the cold gaze of the disturbed leopard that might have been lying along the thick branch above our heads. Every major rustling became the grasses parting before the tiger that could have been stalking our tracks. A sudden and violent crashing sound did in fact occur in the forest to our left, and I stopped dead with my heart leaping into my throat. My mind could picture nothing less than a wild elephant in full charge.

"It is only a family of wild boar," Anandha said. "They can be dangerous, but not when they are running away.

I groped for his shoulder again, feeling somewhat foolish, and again we continued our steady progress. The terrain sloped up, levelled out and then descended again, and I knew we were crossing a ridge. The trees thinned out above us and I looked up to see dim glimmers of starlight, and briefly the feeling of claustrophobia was reduced. Then we were moving into dense tall timber in the valley bottom and the darkness was total again.

We had crossed another ridge and entered a second valley when I heard the alien sound. Anandha and Kueno heard it at the same moment, for we all three froze and listened. It was as though out of the general blanket of insect sound one monstrous wasp was swelling to thunderous volume above the rest. I recognized it as Anandha spoke for the third time.

"It is the helicopter," he said with matter of fact calm.

I stared upwards, seeing nothing, but hearing clearly the metallic clatter of giant rotor blades as the helicopter swept overhead. I remembered Belinda telling me that to remove the larger edifices of masonry a gang of looters would normally use a truck, but in dense jungle such as this a helicopter was obviously the only alternative. The pieces were fitting together, and at this stage it seemed hardly necessary to ask questions of Anandha who had heard the sound before. With my intuition working overtime I felt confident that

I knew the identity of the helicopter pilot.

"Let us hurry," Anandha said, and we followed the fading roar of the invisible whirlybird.

I allowed Anandha's sense of urgency to spur me on, for there could no longer be any doubt that we were on the right trail, and there was an ominous sense of foreboding in my mind. We pressed on faster than before, careless of how many times we stumbled, and then after another mile Anandha insisted that we slow down. He was searching for a sign, and in a faint bar of filtered starlight he found it, a deep, wide gash that he had previously carved in the trunk of a tree.

"Here we leave the path," he said softly. "And from here we must make no noise. It is only a few hundred yards to the place of the secret ruins."

I nodded my understanding, and then he turned sideways and eased his body away from the path. I followed him and found that a passage had been forced on a previous occasion, but I had to reach for his shoulder as the patch of starlight was left behind and we were swallowed in darkness once more. Here the foliage pressed all around us, and the wet tendrils of vegetation enfolded our flinching bodies like the sea depths full of leafy octopi. Kueno's hand closed on my own shoulder, for none of us could now afford to lose contact with the others.

For several minutes Anandha led our blind chain at a snail's pace, guiding us by instinct alone. I began to fear that we were trailing in inevitable circles, but his sense of direction was faultless and finally he stopped, warning us to silence with a murmur that was pitched too low to be broken up into words. I peered over his shoulder, and in the stygian blackness ahead I glimpsed a faint flash of light.

When the warning had been acknowledged we crept forwards again. The lights increased in number, blinking more brightly through the intervening trees, and slowly we heard the sound of voices. Anandha indicated that we should crouch down, and so we sank low and continued towards the source of lights and activity with increased caution.

Slowly the jungle ruins took shape, like pieces of a jigsaw puzzle fitted together by patches of starlight, and the flickering beams of hand-held flashlights. There were three carved stone towers on a single platform, their architectural style more related to India than Thailand, and perhaps indicative of the temple's great age. In addition there were two smaller sanctuaries and a number of shrines, all carved with a great wealth of detail. The whole complex was surrounded by a crumbling wall, and the litter of chopped trees and branches all around showed that it had only recently been hacked free of the strangling jungle.

Amongst those ghostly and decayed remains a large group of men moved like ghouls at an ancient grave. They worked with pickaxes and spades, hammers and chisels, and levers and ropes, and their task was the systematic demolition of the ruins into broken pieces that could be carried away. A massive lintel, carved with a bas-relief motif of leaf garlands and dancing angels was being lowered down from the roof of one of the sanctuaries, and I saw more men carrying a man-sized statue of the God Vishnu from the shambles they were leaving behind. I recognized Samana in his blue headband and the familiar blue and green sarong, standing guard over the rest with his Armalite rifle in his hands. The other members of the gang, I noticed, all had firearms of some sort leaning within easy reach.

In a clearing that had been cut back before the temple ruins stood the helicopter, an American-made Sikorsky Ch-34 Choctaw. I guessed that the interior seats had been ripped out to make more cargo space, for while we watched three of the Thai workers were engaged in hauling up a massive door pillar carved with mythological figures which they dragged inside the fuselage.

The three men in the helicopter were working without any apparent supervision, and I wriggled closer, hoping to get a glimpse of the pilot. I failed to find him, but from my new vantage point I did spot another familiar figure leaning casually against one of the ruined towers. The fat bulk was unmistakable, even though I couldn't see his face. It was Gus Rickhardt and he was tilting his precious whisky flask to his mouth. In his free hand he held another Armalite rifle, and on his head he wore a distinctive green beret. I remembered his boast that he had killed a hundred slit-eyed men in Vietnam, and I guessed that it was there that he had probably looted his first temple. When his military service had ended he had obviously found it profitable to remain in Asia, but safer to continue his pillaging away from the war zones.

For several minutes I lay on my belly and watched the bustle of activity around the ruins. The only sounds were the chink of tools upon stone, and the occasional curse or word of command. I wanted to confirm the identity of the pilot, but the only non-oriental I could see was Rickhardt, and I doubted that he possessed any skill in flying. There was a double slither of movement behind me, and I glanced back and indicated to Anandha and Kueno that they should wait. Alone I wriggled closer to a gap in the main enclosure wall.

I was confident that I could not be seen or heard in the darkness of the jungle night, but it had never occurred to me that Rickhardt might have posted guards outside the perimeter of the temple complex. In this isolated spot in dense jungle that should have been a totally unnecessary precaution, and the first inkling I had that I was in error was when the cold muzzle of a rifle suddenly jabbed down with painful force into my ribs. The guard howled the alarm, and because I had no wish to die an instantaneous death I froze to the damp earth and stopped breathing.

There were more shouts and yells, the sounds of guns being snatched up and bolts clicked back, and then the quick patter of running feet. A dozen flashlights swept through the gap in the wall to pinpoint my prone figure, and not until I heard Gus Rickhardt's harsh chuckle did I dare to relax my muscles and look up.

Rickhardt and Samana were standing over me with levelled rifles, and Rickhardt was showing his broken tooth in a diabolical grin.

"Well if it isn't my little old smart-ass buddy! We've been expecting you for the last hour. You've kept all the boys waiting."

I began to understand why he had posted the unexpected guard, and when they allowed me to get up and shoved me towards the temple courtyard my understanding became crystal clear. The helicopter pilot had at last shown his face and was standing in the doorway to one of the sanctuaries. In his right hand he held a Colt 0.45 automatic, and on his face the old amiable grin appeared to be frozen at the edges.

"I brought Gus the warning, David. You see, I figured that you just had to show your face here." Jack Holden paused for a moment and then added. "I also flew out some extra insurance, just to guarantee your good behaviour."

He reached into the temple doorway and dragged Tracey Ryan out beside him. The black snout of the automatic he pushed hard against her white throat.

"So you had just better behave, David Chan," he finished bluntly. "Because I'm not so damned besotted with your lovely friend here that I wouldn't blow her head off if you made it necessary!"

19

I HEARD more movement from behind, and looked back with a sinking heart to see Anandha and Kueno emerging from the black barrier of the jungle with their hands raised and more rifles jabbing them forward. The guard who had trapped me so neatly had not been alone, and it seemed that Rickhardt must have posted at least six of his armed Thais well back in the tree line. They had been given advance warning, and had simply waited in silence for us to wriggle through their ranks before they had pounced from behind.

I looked back to the doorway of the temple sanctuary. Tracey was flushed and angry and her red hair was awry. She was standing awkwardly on one foot to ease the weight from her lame ankle. There was more pain than fear in her eyes, and despite the automatic boring into her throat she managed a bitter apology.

"I'm sorry, David. He didn't give me a lot of choice."

"It's alright." I controlled my voice carefully and shifted my glance to Holden. "How did you figure it all out, Jack?"

He grinned. "You might say it was simple deduction, one step leading to another. For a start I figured that the two guys in the dance costumes just had to be Kueno and his brother. Those two have been sneaking around our operation for a long time, but until now we haven't been able to catch them at it. When they tried to kill you they must have thought that you were one of us, but it was obvious that if you caught up with them and started talking then all that misunderstanding would get sorted out. And once you did get it sorted out it seemed obvious that from there you would pool all your knowledge and team up, and Kueno and his brother would lead you here."

"It was a fairly simple line of deduction," I admitted bleakly.

Holden nodded, he had complete control of the situation and his grin began to thaw a little.

"Naturally when Belinda and Tracey came back to the hotel and told me that you and the two dancers had just vanished into the night, I knew they had to be lying. They didn't show enough concern, David. I've noticed that they are quite fond of you, and if you had gone missing without a trace they would have been busting a gut to find you. The fact that they were not worried meant that you were okay, and because I knew that you wouldn't give up the chase it could only mean that you had caught up with these guys and become pals. After a while I got Tracey alone and tried to sweet-talk her into giving me the truth. She wouldn't, but she wasn't fooling me either, so finally I just stuck a gun against her head and brought her along."

"You were lucky," I said. "You made guesses and they all proved to be right."

"Don't get sour. I'm just a better detective than you are."

"That's almost true." So many things were becoming clear that I was inclined to agree with him. "You told me that you were in the U.S. Air Force, but I never gave that enough thought. Did you ever fly a Thunderchief, or was it always helicopters?"

"I was always a chopper pilot. You can kick yourself, David, because you only needed to check with Chieng Mai airport and you would have found out that I fly a helicopter charter service throughout Thailand. I have to fly some legitimate cargoes to cover this job. That part was always wide open — it's my connection with Srivaji that should have been secret."

"And Rickhardt was in the Special Forces," I said. "He still wears the green beret, but I should have guessed when he bragged about killing Vietnamese. The two of you teamed up in Vietnam."

Holden nodded. "Gus brought back the occasional relic from the temples his unit found on some of their missions. I found a buyer for those pieces in Srivaji. Later I found out about the Srivaji-Sanders tie-up, and the fact that they were already using that pottery factory to disguise art works and smuggle them out of Thailand. The outlet was already there for everything that Gus and I could find, so I just bought us in and expanded the business."

"You're telling him too much, Jack," Rickhardt warned harshly.

"It doesn't matter," Holden said. "Because he isn't leaving here alive. All three of these guys have become much too troublesome anyway."

He stopped for a moment, and then spoke in Thai to Samana. The wrinkle-faced Thai nodded with unquestioning approval, and then he and half a dozen of his companions slowly raised their rifles. Samana prodded me sharply with the muzzle of his Armalite M-16. I saw that Anandha and Kueno were already being forced to move back towards the trees, and it was obvious that we were being herded into the jungle and shot.

"So long, David," Holden said calmly.

I stared at him for another second. He still had that Colt 0.45 pressed against Tracey's throat, and there was nothing that she or I could do to prevent his orders from being carried out. I couldn't meet Tracey's agonized eyes, and so I turned away.

Gus Rickhardt gave me a leering grin but I ignored him. If I had to die then I preferred it to be out of Tracey's sight and I began to walk slowly towards the black wall of the forest.

At the same time my brain raced with far-flung hopes. Perhaps Samana would stumble, or perhaps there would be an opportunity to let a branch spring back into his face as we entered the trees.

Samana was sure-footed and wary and I knew that I didn't have a real chance in hell, but I was determined to try. My heart was pounding and my hands sweated, and my nerve ends were wound up in knots ready to explode. The darkness of the forest was the darkness of death, and with each step it was beginning to embrace me. It was all over, and I had only my final seconds to decide whether to attempt to dodge and run before taking that lethal burst of bullets in the back. I could sense that Samana was ready to increase the pressure in his trigger finger, and then like a sword stroke a ringing command in Thai cut through the pregnant night.

Samana jerked towards the sound. I felt the muzzle of the Armalite swing away from my spine and my bunched muscles uncoiled in a desperate spring in the opposite direction. I hit the ground and rolled frantically, while behind me the Armalite crashed out a burst of fire that almost drowned the one sharp crack from a police revolver.

My shoulder smashed into a tree trunk and I came to an abrupt stop. I looked back and saw Samana reeling and the M-16 falling from his grasp. Beyond him, emerging from the forest gloom, was a brisk, half-crouched figure which I recognized by the peaked cap. There was a further exchange of savage gunfire, but Karachorn was well supported by a squad of armed policeman moving rapidly out of the jungle, and it was the two men driving Kueno and Anandha who screamed and fell.

The remainder of the gang still grouped in the precincts of the temple made a brief resistance. A few of them dived for cover behind the ruined walls, but mostly they were caught in the glare of the lights that they themselves had rigged up in order to work by night. The police had the twin advantages of surprise and the cover of darkness. Shots rang out on all sides, but quickly the defenders began to throw their weapons away and raise their hands.

Only Rickhardt and Holden made positive moves. Rickhardt grabbed the nearest of his own men, and using the struggling wretch as a living shield began to back away rapidly between two of the ancient towers. Holden already had Tracey in his grasp and he followed Rickhardt's example. At the same time he fired off two wild shots from his Colt automatic at the advancing police forces.

The moment that the Colt was removed from her throat I saw Tracey's red head flash round. She followed the movement of the gun and sank her white teeth deep into the knuckle of Holden's thumb. He howled in anger and then made an effort to throw her away. Her sprained ankle collapsed beneath her and she fell heavily in the temple doorway. As she sprawled helpless Holden saw that his last chance had gone and in vengeful fury he levelled the Colt at her heart.

I was on my feet and running madly, but there wasn't a hope that I could reach him before he pulled the trigger. Mercifully he paused to curse her, and in that moment Karachorn shouted from my right.

"Chan!"

As I heard my name my head whipped round. I saw that Karachorn was also running forward but that part of the ruined temple wall was blocking his line of fire. He threw the big police revolver neatly towards me, and there was a horrible second when I thought that it was going to miss my hand. For an eternity the weapon seemed to sail through the starlight, but his aim was accurate and my grip didn't fumble. The butt of the revolver smacked into my palm, and I closed my fist and jerked the trigger as I took aim. My shot was the first by a split second, and Jack Holden spun round and toppled off the edge of the temple platform.

Rickhardt was the only danger left.

He had retreated between the two towers, but he was having difficulty in holding on to the luckless Thai he had dragged along as a shield, and was unable to use the Armalite M-16 that was still gripped in his right hand. I rushed towards him and in the same moment he stumbled backwards over a broken pile of fallen masonry. He was forced to release his prisoner and fumbled to bring up the M-16. In that same second I collided heavily with Anandha.

"Please?"

Anandha spoke only the one word, and I remembered that Rickhardt was the murderer of his brother Muang. He didn't need me, and so I stood aside and watched.

Rickhardt almost had the M-16 into a firing position when Anandah reached him. The young Thai kicked him straight in the face and Rickhardt was bowled over backwards, the rifle flying out of his hands. Anandha stopped then and waited. Rickhardt clawed himself up with blood flowing from his nose. He let out a roar that was as savage as his face and blundered forward. If he had succeeded in getting a grip on his slimmer opponent he could have broken Anandha's back with his bare hands, but those hands never found their mark. Anandha twisted deftly to one side, turned and delivered another flying high kick that rocked Rickhardt just under the heart. While the big American floundered wildly Anandha hit him with a straight right cross that opened up a cut above his eye, and from then on their fight became a two fisted massacre. Rickhardt staggered helplessly, blinded by his own blood, while Anandha attacked and mercilessly cut the bigger man to pieces.

When Rickhardt measured his own length in the dust for the third time Karachorn reluctantly sent his men to intervene.

"We must save something for the trial," he said.

I nodded, and returned his revolver.

He accepted it with a beaming smile and then went forward to assist his men.

★ ★ ★

I turned away and found that Belinda had appeared with the main wave of policemen. She and Kueno were helping Tracey to get up, and I was relieved to see them all looking unharmed. I spared a glance for Jack Holden who was now sitting on the ground and clasping his blood-stained shoulder. He was flanked by two policemen and the look he gave me was one of black hate.

"Thanks for coming," I said quietly to Belinda.

She smiled faintly. "It was an awkward decision, David. I knew that Jack was suspicious, and when he disappeared with Tracey I knew that something was wrong. I felt instinctively that if he was emerging in his true colours then he would be making his way here to intercept you. I finally took the whole story to Inspector Karachorn, and he armed half the Chieng Mai police force. We dashed to Chandi in a fleet of police cars, and there the old priest found us guides to bring us here."

Karachorn came to join us.

"Miss Carrington made the wise decision," he said precisely. "We arrived only just in time, but now we have smashed this gang of temple robbers, and I am sure that I shall have enough evidence to arrest Mister Srivaji when I return to Bangkok. All very satisfactory."

"Not all," Tracey said. We all looked towards her and she continued: "David, surely you haven't forgotten that this investigation started as a murder enquiry — and we still don't know who murdered Mark Sanders."

In the silence that followed I was about to concede that she was right, but then Belinda declared quietly.

"That's a debatable point." She had

regained our attention and she went on to explain: "This morning David asked me to send an urgent cable to Hong Kong. I did so and received the answer tonight. In fact it was the arrival of the cable that prompted me to look for Tracey. I expected to find her in the bedroom resting that ankle, but of course I found instead that she was missing."

"But what was in the cable?" Karachorn asked with interest.

"It was the answer to a request. David wanted to know whether Holden, Srivaji or Rickhardt could have been in Hong Kong at the time of the Sanders murder. Superintendent Davies replied with a negative for all three, but there is one man present who was in Hong Kong at that time." She gazed frankly at Karachorn. "That man was you, Inspector. You landed at Kai Tak Airport twenty-four hours before Mark Sanders died, and you departed on a return flight to Bangkok just twelve hours after the murder."

Karachorn smiled his admiration, while I regretted that I had returned his revolver which he still held casually in his right hand.

"So that's the final answer," I said quietly. "You're a cultured man, Inspector. You were angry at the way this gang had been plundering your country of its past. You couldn't prove a case against Srivaji, or anyone else at this end, but you were prepared to smash open the Hong Kong end by committing murder."

To my surprise Karachorn calmly shook his head.

"No, Mister Chan. It is true that I paid an unofficial visit to Hong Kong in connection with this case. But I only went to visit the two branches of *Exotic Art* in the hope that I might discover any stolen art works. I could not confirm my suspicions and so I returned to Bangkok. I assure you that I did not kill Mark Sanders."

I stared at him, but his round face was placid and totally lacking in guile, and after a moment I believed him.

I turned my reproving gaze on Anandha who had also drawn close to listen.

"You lied to me," I said sadly.

"No!" He denied the charge. "I have told you before that the man Sanders was already dead when I arrived at the villa, and I will swear to it again."

I stared at him in turn, and the crazy thing was that I believed him too. I was baffled, and then Belinda chuckled softly.

"There was more in that cable, David. I held it back just in case Ray had made a mistake, but now I have no more doubts. Ten hours ago the Hong Kong police arrested Mister Wang, the manager of the Kowloon branch of *Exotic Art*, for the murder of his employer. It seems that Wang went to the villa to demand a raise in salary, and because he knew that Sanders was dealing in stolen goods he coupled the demand with blackmail. They quarrelled, and Wang killed Sanders in a fit of rage."

Karachorn looked pleased, while Anandha looked puzzled, and I felt completely and permanently deflated.

"I'm sure we'll find that Srivaji warned Sanders to be on his guard because of the danger from Anandha and Keuno. That would account for the extra precautions that Sanders was taking before he died. However, it was Wang who committed the murder, and Sanders had no reason to beware of Wang until the moment they both lost their tempers." Belinda concluded her story with an apologetic smile. "I'm sorry, David, but this time we were all on the wrong track. The killer never left Hong Kong, and the police have wrapped up the case in our absence."

There was a moment of wry silence, and then Karachorn gave me some cheer.

"You may not have solved your murder case, Mister Chan, but you have helped to smash a gang of very dangerous temple thieves. For that, I can assure you, Thailand is exceedingly grateful."

Belinda gave me a warm consolation kiss, and Tracey did the same, and with that I had to be satisfied. I put my arms around them both and accepted their ministrations of comfort with philosophical calm.

THE END

Other titles in the Linford Mystery Library:

A GENTEEL LITTLE MURDER
Philip Daniels

Gilbert had a long-cherished plan to murder his wife. When the polished Edward entered the scene Gilbert's attitude was suddenly changed.

DEATH AT THE WEDDING
Madelaine Duke

Dr. Norah North's search for a killer takes her from a wedding to a private hospital.

MURDER FIRST CLASS
Ron Ellis

Will Detective Chief Inspector Glass find the Post Office robbers before the Executioner gets to them?